CLAIMING HIS BROTHER'S BABY

BY
HELEN LACEY

Published in Great Britain 2015
by Mills & Boon, an imprint of Harlequin (UK) Limited,
Eton House, 18-24 Paradise Road, Richmond, Surrey, TW9 1SR

© 2015 Helen Lacey

ISBN: 978-0-263-25102-9

23-0115

Harlequin (UK) Limited's policy is to use papers that are natural, renewable and recyclable products and made from wood grown in sustainable forests. The logging and manufacturing processes conform to the legal environmental regulations of the country of origin.

Printed and bound in Spain
by CPI, Barcelona

Helen Lacey grew up reading *Black Beauty* and *Little House on the Prairie*. These childhood classics inspired her to write her first book when she was seven, a story about a girl and her horse. She loves writing for Mills & Boon® Cherish™, where she can create strong heroes with a soft heart and heroines with gumption who get their happily-ever-after. For more about Helen, visit her website, www.helenlacey.com.

For Nani
Because big sisters really are the best!

Chapter One

Cassie Duncan placed her four-month-old son in his bed and gently rubbed his belly through the pale blue cotton onesie. Oliver's breathing slowed and she watched his tiny chest rise and fall, marveling at the perfect little person who'd come into her life.

If only your daddy was here...

But Doug was gone. Killed eight months earlier while on tour in the Middle East, he never got to see his son born. Now it was just the two of them, getting through each day. Cassie adored being a mother and loved Oliver more than she'd imagined she could love anyone. But she was sad that Doug would miss seeing his son grow up. He'd had very little family, just a younger brother in South Dakota he rarely saw. And Crystal Point was a long way from there. With a population of eight hundred, the small Australian beachside town sat at the southernmost point of the Great Barrier Reef. It was the perfect place to raise her child—quiet and safe—a place where she fit in, where she led a valuable life.

She grabbed the baby monitor, flicked on the colored shaded night-light and left the nursery. Mouse hunkered down the hall when he saw her. The one-hundred-and-sixty-pound black-and-white Great Dane always stood point at the end of the hall when she was in the nursery with Oliver. The dog pushed his big head against her leg and Cassie rubbed his neck.

"Feel like a snack?" she asked and kept walking.

Mouse followed her through to the kitchen. She gave him a couple of doggy treats and filled up the kettle. Oliver would stay asleep for a few hours, so she had time to make dinner and watch a movie. She rummaged through the pantry and settled on tinned soup and sourdough toast. The dog climbed into his bed by the door and Cassie set about making her meal.

Friday nights always seemed the quietest somehow. In the old days she would have called her best friends, Lauren and Mary-Jayne, to come around and they would have opened a bottle of wine and eaten cheese and crackers and shared stories about their week. But Lauren was recently engaged and making wedding plans with her fiancé. And Mary-Jayne was locked away in her workshop and wouldn't be around for a week.

And I have Oliver.

Having a baby had changed her priorities. Not that Cassie had ever been much of a party girl. She'd dated Doug for three years before his death and although they hadn't seen much of one another in the last eighteen months, she had stood by her commitment to their relationship. Being involved with a career soldier had been difficult. However, the long absences and constant worry for his safety hadn't altered her feelings. She'd loved him, and now she loved their son.

She cranked the lid off the soup tin, poured it into a saucepan and sliced some bread while she waited for the soup to heat up. The baby monitor was quiet and Cassie relaxed when she sat down at the big scrubbed table and ate her dinner. The house was silent, except for its usual creaks and moans. But she loved the house and had lived in it for most of her life.

When her grandfather had fallen ill four years ago and needed full-time care, the house had been sold to an investment buyer to pay for his care and she had become a tenant in her own home. Of course she was grateful to have been able to stay on and lease the property from the new owner.

The new owner had turned out to be Doug and when he briefly returned from his tour and came around to check on the house, they'd quickly fallen for one another. There weren't fireworks or a rush of crazy heat, but they'd shared something more…something lasting. It was grounded in friendship and Cassie would have happily spent her life with him had fate not intervened. But only months after she'd told him she was pregnant Doug was dead, killed by a sniper in a secret operation along with two other soldiers.

She'd been living in the house ever since, paying the rent and utilities, and had begrudgingly started looking for another place to live while waiting for the home she loved to be pulled out from under her and Oliver.

Because the house now belonged to Doug's brother, Tanner McCord. She'd met him twice and on both occasions he'd proven to be the disinterested, brooding loner Doug had described. She knew the tension between the two men went back a long way and whenever she'd asked Doug about it he'd quickly dismissed her questions. Now all she could do was wait until she learned what Tanner planned to do with the house. Eight days earlier she'd received an email. He was coming back to Crystal Point. He wanted to see her. He wanted to talk.

He wants to kick me out of my home...

Cassie shuddered. Damn. She should be better prepared. She should have found somewhere else to live. She should have contacted a lawyer again and ascertained whether Oliver had any rights to Doug's estate. Instead, she'd buried her head in the sand, plastered on her regular happy smile and hoped things would work out. Like a naive fool. As always.

She shook off the unease in her blood and finished her meal. Once she'd eaten and washed up, she left the kitchen, checked the baby, gathered her things and headed for the bathroom. Twenty minutes later she was showered, dried and wearing her comfiest gray sweats. By seven she was in front of the television watching a DVD.

But not even her favorite romantic comedy could hold her attention. She'd had a headache all afternoon, amplified by the increasing funk she'd been in since Tanner's email had arrived. She was nervous. On edge and restless at the idea of facing him without Doug by her side. And she felt...alone. Something she hadn't truly experienced since her parents had died. Or since her grandfather had gone into the nursing home. Even when she didn't see Doug for months at a time she hadn't labored over being alone. This was something else. Something more. Cassie couldn't figure why the feeling was so intense. Since Oliver's birth she hadn't any time to linger over what she had lost, or the life she'd never have with Doug. But tonight the feelings were acute. Tonight she was *lonely.*

When her parents had died in a boating accident Cassie had gone to live with her grandfather Neville Duncan. She'd been eight years old and had grieved the loss of her family for a long time. Lauren's folks had helped, and her granddad had done his best. But it wasn't like having a family, a mother and father, of her own. With Doug she'd hoped that together they would make a family. But that wasn't to be. Still, she was determined to tell her son everything she knew about his father. Doug wouldn't be forgotten.

As for Tanner…she'd deal with whatever happened.

I can make this work.

I have to.

It was dark out and Tanner McCord had been sitting in the car for over half an hour.

Waiting.

And knowing he should have let the lawyers handle it instead of traveling halfway around the world to see her. They were only connected by her child. Doug's son. The son his brother would never see.

Tanner drummed his fingers on the steering wheel. It had been over two years since he'd seen her. And that was only the second time since she'd become involved with Doug. But now Doug was gone. And Tanner was home to fulfill the unspoken promise he'd made to his brother.

He looked toward the house. A silhouette passed by a window. Tanner's stomach lurched and he sucked in a deep breath. His leg ached and he pressed his palm hard into his left thigh. After months of rehab he could finally walk without that damn stick. The pain was worse when he drove for a length of time, and the five-hour haul from Brisbane to Crystal Point after twenty-plus hours in the air crossing the Pacific had taken its toll. He mostly avoided pain meds in favor of massage and physical therapy, but right now needed something to take his mind off the soreness and maintain his focus. Tanner popped a couple of aspirin and waited for the pain to ease as it usually did when he put pressure on the main fracture line.

There was more movement by the window, followed by a light being switched on in the front room. The big, low-set brick-and-tile home was positioned well back from the road and in the fading dusk he'd noticed how overgrown and unkempt the garden was. Tanner could see the flickering light from the television bouncing shadows off the curtains and he wondered if he should wait until morning before disturbing her.

Instead, he got out, pushing past the pain in his leg, and closed the door. Tanner walked across the curb and stalled in the middle of the driveway. Driving for hours had exaggerated his limp and he pulled his leg forward to force a straight stride. When he reached the door he knocked twice and waited. Seconds later he heard the soft sound of feet padding over floorboards before the door opened back on its hinges.

Cassandra.

His stomach rolled again. She was beautiful, as he remembered. Hair the color of treacle, pale blue eyes, porcelain skin and soft, even features. The first time Doug had introduced her to him, Tanner's breath had been sucked from his chest. The second time he was better prepared—he managed a quick visit while Doug was home on leave and had kept his distance from her. And this time…this time he had his head screwed on right. He wasn't in Crystal Point to lust over his dead brother's girlfriend.

History would not repeat itself. Not ever again.

"Tanner?"

She said his name in that soft, breathless way and a familiar jolt of awareness rushed through his blood. He finally drew in some air and spoke. "Hello, Cassandra."

Her gaze narrowed as a huge dog moved around her legs

and sniffed the air. The animal eyed him suspiciously and lifted his ears in alert mode. She certainly looked as though she had all the protection she needed. "You're here…"

"You got my email?"

"Ah…yes…but I wasn't expecting you until next week."

"I got an earlier flight," he explained and pressed down the jolt of pain contracting his thigh. "I'm sorry if I startled you. I probably should have called first."

She looked flustered and a little put out, and guilt twitched Tanner behind his shoulder blades. He should have waited until morning. Or he should have let the lawyers handle it.

"No, it's fine," she said and nodded. "You can come inside."

When she opened the screen and stepped back Tanner moved through the doorway. She closed both doors behind him and suggested they go into the living room. The dog trailed her and Tanner hung back for a moment. He finally followed her down the hall and remained by the doorway when she entered the front room.

Tanner watched her. She looked cautious. On edge. Out of sorts.

Suspicious.

The room had altered a little since the last time he'd been in it. There was some new furniture, new rug, different paintings on the walls. There was a fireplace with one of those fake heaters and a photo on the mantel caught his attention. Doug. In uniform. The face seemed as recognizable as it did unfamiliar. When he was young he'd worshipped Doug.

But things had a way of changing.

"That's quite an animal you have there," he said.

"Mouse," she replied and ushered the dog to sit on a rug

near the fireplace. The animal gave Tanner a wary once-over before curling on the mat.

"Mouse?"

She smiled a little. "The idea was to make him seem less intimidating."

When the dog was settled, Tanner crossed the threshold. "How are you?"

She nodded. "Fine."

"And the—your son?"

"Oliver," she said, as though he didn't know the child's name. "He's asleep."

He took a few steps and noticed how her gaze fell to his uneven gait. She knew about the accident that had laid him up in hospital for over a month. It was the reason he hadn't made it to Doug's funeral.

"And are you well?" he asked and moved behind the heavy sofa.

"I said I was." She looked him over. "More the point, how are *you*?"

Tanner tapped his thigh. "Better. Good as new."

Her brows came up. "Really?"

He shrugged. "Maybe not exactly like new. But I'm getting there."

"I should have called," she said quietly. "But after Doug…you know…and the baby came…and by then I didn't have time to think about anything but Oliver."

He understood. And he hadn't expected her to call. They weren't friends. They weren't anything. She was Doug's woman. The mother of his brother's child. It didn't matter that her blue eyes and soft smile invaded his dreams. Wanting her was pointless. He'd never act on it, never give in to it. Never put himself through the inevitable humiliation of her rejection. Staying in South Dakota and living his life far away from her and Doug had been the sensible option.

"It's okay, Cassandra. You don't have to—"

"Cassie," she said, correcting him. "No one calls me Cassandra."

Tanner lingered over the thought. He'd always called her that. Funny how he'd never picked up that she didn't like it. "All right…Cassie."

She smiled a little and sat on the sofa. "Would you like coffee? Tea?"

"No, thank you."

"You can sit down if you want."

He nodded and moved farther into the room. She watched him intently as he eased into the opposite chair and stretched out his left leg. She couldn't have missed the way he favored the one side when he walked.

"Are you in pain?" she asked.

Tanner shrugged. "It was a long trip."

The suspicion in her gaze didn't abate. "You said in your email that you wanted to talk. So, what did you want to talk about?"

In normal circumstances it might not have sounded like a fraught, loaded question. But nothing about the situation was normal. And they both knew it.

"Don't look so wary, Cassie. I would have been here eight months ago if it hadn't been for the accident. I finally got the all clear to travel and came as soon as I could."

"For what?" she asked quietly, but she was clearly on edge. "Doug's dead. Anything that needs to be sorted could be done through lawyers."

Silence stretched between them like frayed elastic. *She doesn't want me here.* He ignored her mention of lawyers. There was time to get to all of that. "You're right," he said, consciously keeping his voice light. "Doug is gone. But his son is very much alive."

Her pale eyes widened. "You came to see Oliver?"

"Of course."

"Why?"

Tanner sucked in a heavy breath. "Because he's the only family that I have."

Family.

Cassie almost choked out a sob the way he said the word. She longed for Oliver to have a family. But this man was a stranger. Unknown. Someone she'd met a couple of times and who had always managed to unnerve her even though they'd barely spoken. She wasn't sure why, but knew it wasn't simply a reaction to his handsome face. There was something about Tanner…something that almost felt familiar…as if they were connected somehow. It was stupid, of course. There was no connection…no common link other than Doug.

Still…he was extraordinarily handsome—dark brown hair, eyes the color of warm toffee and he possessed a strong, muscular frame. Features that made him impossible to ignore. He was taller than Doug had been, and leaner in the waist and hips and broader through the shoulders. He was the kind of man who'd look good in jeans, chambray shirt and cowboy boots, or a suit and tie.

Tanner McCord was gorgeous, no doubt about it. But she wasn't about to get caught up in his good looks. She took a deep breath and spoke. "I didn't realize family was so important to you."

It was a direct dig and he obviously knew it. "Doug and I had different lives," he said and stretched back against the chair. "Which doesn't mean we didn't care about each other."

"I know how Doug felt about you," she replied carefully. "He told me how he looked after you when your parents died."

Tanner's eyes darkened. "He did, that's right. I was nine years old. Doug was twenty-one. I lived with him for three months before he joined the army."

Cassie frowned. She knew Tanner was about to turn thirty-one and born the same year she was. "I thought Doug went into the army when he was twenty-three?"

There was another stretch of silence, longer this time, as though he was working out how to answer her. "No. Twenty-one."

"And where did you live then?"

"Boarding school," he replied. "He visited when he could."

It wasn't quite the story she'd heard. Doug hadn't mentioned sending his younger brother away to school at such a young age. "Well, of course he would do that, being Doug," she said, and ignored the tiny stab of disapproval tapping in her head. "So, how long are you staying in town?"

"Awhile."

How long was "awhile"? "To see Oliver?"

"If that's okay?"

She wondered how her cheerful, lovable son would take to the man whose eyes were just like his own. *No, they're Doug's eyes.* But she didn't have any reason to refuse his request. "You can see him tomorrow."

"Thank you, Cassie."

She looked at the clock on the mantel. It was nearly eight o'clock. Early. Probably too early to send him on his way. "So, you're staying in Bellandale?"

The town, with its sixty thousand residents, was twenty minutes away from the small beachside community of Crystal Point and had many quality hotels.

"Yeah, I'm sure I'll find a hotel."

Cassie frowned and tried not to think about how his

soft accent seemed to warm her skin. "You didn't book a hotel room?"

He shrugged. "I'll find somewhere. I picked up a rental car at the airport. I was born in Bellandale, remember? I know my way around town."

She did know. In fact they'd been born at the same hospital, barely a week apart. But they had never met until after she'd started dating Doug. "So, about ten tomorrow?"

"Sure," he said and got to his feet.

Cassie noticed the slight wobble and how he pushed down hard on his right leg. He was obviously in pain. She didn't know much about his accident, only that it had been life threatening and something to do with a horse. Now wasn't the time to ask. And really, the less she knew the better. Tanner wasn't part of her life. Nor did she want him to be.

She was just about to say good-night and walk him out when he faltered on his feet and quickly gripped the back of the sofa for support. Cassie rushed forward. "Are you okay?"

"Fine," he said and grimaced. "Damn leg locks up sometimes. It'll pass."

Cassie wasn't so sure. He looked pale and uncomfortable. The long drive to Crystal Point that had followed an even longer flight from South Dakota had clearly caught up with him. "Are you sure you can drive?"

He shrugged fractionally. "I guess I'll find out. Good night, Cassie."

She watched as he took a slow step, then another. He was in tremendous pain and trying not to show it. "Tanner?" His name fell from her lips.

"Yes?"

What am I doing?

"You…you could stay here tonight," she said quietly and

couldn't quite believe the words were coming out. But she didn't want him driving and potentially crashing. He was Doug's brother. Oliver's uncle. Old-fashioned consideration surged through her. "You're not exactly in any condition to drive. And you said you'll be coming back to see Oliver tomorrow anyway. And since you haven't booked into a hotel. I think… I think…"

What? Having him spend the night is a good idea? In what stratosphere?

"You think what?"

She shrugged lightly. Okay, maybe it wasn't a good idea. But he *was* Oliver's uncle. And family, in a way. Plus, technically the house was his. He had every right to stay.

"It was just an idea. You look tired and in pain, that's all. And there are two spare rooms. But if you'd rather go to a—"

"If you're sure," he said, cutting her off.

She wasn't sure about anything. Especially when it came to Tanner McCord. "Of course."

He watched her, rattling her nerves in that way he always seemed to do. "Then I'll stay. And you're right, Cassie, I'm beat. I'd really like a shower and some sleep. Thank you."

So it was settled. He was staying.

"I'll show you to your room," she said quietly and forced some air into her lungs.

"I'll get my bag. Be back in a minute."

She told Mouse to stay put, walked from the room and up the hall and waited while Tanner headed back outside. He returned in a few minutes with a battered duffel draped over one strong shoulder. He wore dark jeans and a long-sleeved black shirt with piping around the pocket and cuffs and, despite the now pronounced effort as he walked, Cassie felt a sharp niggle of awareness way down low. That he could do that to her, despite how much she had loved Doug, always made her resent him just that little bit more than she would have liked.

"This way," she said and walked down the hall. He followed and stood in the doorway once she entered the bedroom. "The sheets are fresh and there are spare towels hanging in the bathroom."

"Thank you," he said as he walked into the room and dropped his bag at the foot of the bed.

"Well, I'll leave you to it. I need to check on Oliver."

Cassie left the room as swiftly as she could and headed for the nursery, and tried not to think about how she suddenly had a man staying in her spare room.

His spare room. His house.

With a heavy heart it occurred to her she was now a visitor in her own home.

Once she'd checked on the baby Cassie made it to the kitchen and turned on the kettle. She heard the shower running and tried to concentrate on making tea. The wall clock read just past eight-thirty and she hoped once Tanner had showered he'd give in to the jet lag and crash out for the night.

But not so.

Fifteen minutes later he appeared in the doorway. He wore low-rise, loose-fitting jeans and a white Henley shirt that did little to disguise the washboard belly and broad shoulders. His hair was damp and flopped over his forehead.

So, he's as sexy as sin.

It wasn't exactly a news flash. The first time she'd met Tanner she'd been aware of his many physical attributes. Doug had joked how his brother had gotten all the looks in the family. Not that he'd been unattractive, but he certainly hadn't possessed the classic handsomeness of the man now hovering in the doorway.

"Tea?" she asked and tried not to think about how the air seemed suddenly thicker.

He shrugged. "Coffee?"

Cassie nodded and grabbed a couple of mugs. "Is instant okay?" she asked. "Or I can put the percolator on for—"

"Instant is fine," he said easily.

She relaxed a little and began making the coffee. "Now that you've showered and changed do you feel human again?"

"Yeah. I don't mind flying, but I always seem to get a chronic case of jet lag."

"Doug loved flying," she said as she poured his coffee and then sugared her tea. She remembered that Tanner liked his coffee with only a little milk. *Funny how some memories stuck.*

"My brother always was the adventurous one."

Cassie didn't quite believe that. While Doug had joined the army and made a career as a soldier, she knew Tanner had traveled the world before settling in South Dakota to work his special kind of magic with horses. He had the swagger and confidence of a man who knew who he was. Now she wondered how much the accident had changed his life and the work he loved.

"Can you still ride?" she asked, figuring there were things that had to be said and she needed time to work up to the hard questions.

"Not yet," he replied and came farther into the room.

Cassie glanced up. "When you called to say you couldn't come to the funeral because you were in hospital I kind of zoned out and didn't ask many questions about what had happened to you. I think I was still in shock at the time."

"Understandable," he said and walked around the table.

He pulled out a chair and sat down. "I was in a bit of shock myself. I guess I always thought Doug was invincible." He tapped his leg in a kind of ironic gesture "Turns out, no one is."

Cassie brought the mugs to the table and sat down. "So, what happened?"

"You mean the accident? I got in the way of a frightened horse and was trampled."

It sounded oversimplified and she raised her brows. "And?"

"A busted leg, broken wrist, four fractured ribs and concussion. Cuts and abrasions. And I lost my spleen."

"A horse did that?" she asked, horrified by the seriousness of his injuries.

He sipped his coffee. "I was at a friend's ranch. His young daughter got between the colt and the fence and I pulled her out of the way. But I wasn't quick enough to make it back through the corral gate. The horse struck me in the chest and once I was down that was it. There was nothing anyone could have done."

Cassie's throat tightened. "You could have been killed."

He shrugged lightly. "I spent a month in hospital and the next six working to get back on my feet."

"It happened only a few days or so before Doug died," she said quietly, thinking of the irony. "It must have been hard for you, being in hospital and getting the news your brother was gone."

He shrugged again, but Cassie wasn't fooled. There was something in his expression that told her losing his brother had been shattering. She'd always thought Tanner to be aloof and insensitive. Doug had called him a free spirit, the kind of man who would never settle down, never lay down roots. But she wasn't so sure. She decided to ask him.

There was no point in being coy. There was too much at stake. "What are you really doing here, Tanner?"

He sat back slowly in his seat and watched her. "I told you."

"To see your nephew?" It seemed too easy. Too simple.

"That's right."

"How long are you staying?"

He pushed the mug aside. "I'm not sure."

Cassie's back stiffened. "Then I have to ask you," she said and pushed her shoulders back. "Are you kicking us out of this house?"

Chapter Two

Tanner had expected the question. He knew she'd want to know about the house. It had to be hard for her. She'd lived in the house since she was a child. When her grandfather's health had declined, the house was put on the market and sold…to Doug. Tanner had no idea why his brother had bought the place. But he knew Cassie had a deep connection to the home she'd once shared with her grandfather.

"Of course not."

She let out a long breath, as though she'd been holding it. He noticed her knuckles were white around the mug. "Oh, okay."

"This is still your home, Cassie."

"But Doug—"

Tanner straightened his spine. "It's still your home," he said again, firmer this time.

"For the moment. And according to Doug's lawyer, the house belongs to you."

"An oversight, obviously."

It wasn't the truth. It wasn't even close to it. But Tanner wouldn't divulge that knowledge. There was no point. Doug was dead. His brother had left a mess behind—one Tanner had to clean up before he returned to South Dakota.

"I don't understand what you mean."

He lied again. "I'm sure Doug had every intention of—"

"I'm not sure what Doug intended," she said, cutting him off.

But Tanner did. Doug had made his thoughts about the house and the child Cassie carried very clear. He drank some coffee and looked at her. She was so effortlessly pretty. His insides stirred and he quickly pushed the thought aside.

"It makes no difference now."

She shook her head. "But the house —"

"It has a mortgage," he said quietly. "Did you know that?"

She shook her head again. "I wasn't sure. Doug never talked about it much when he returned from tour. I've been paying rent and the utilities like I've done since he first bought the place." She stopped and looked at him. "How large a mortgage?"

His stomach tightened as he named the figure.

"Oh…that's…that's a lot."

It *was* a lot. It was a six-figure hole that wouldn't be covered by Doug's insurance policy. Most of the money had gone to repay the balance on three maxed credit cards and a bank loan taken out to purchase the top-of-the-range Ducati stored in the garage.

He pushed down the resentment thickening his blood. Whatever Doug had done, Tanner had come to Crystal Point to fix things…not make matters worse. And definitely not to upset the woman who'd borne his brother's child.

"We'll talk about it tomorrow," he said gently, trying to put her at ease.

"I'd rather—"

"Tomorrow," he said again and stood, scraping the chair back. "I think I should crash before the jet lag really takes hold."

"Okay. Good night."

"'Night, Cassie."

He left the room quickly and ten minutes later he was asleep. Only his dreams were plagued by images of pale blue eyes and soft lips. And memories of the girl he'd met so long ago, but who didn't remember him.

Cassie got up during the night to feed and change the baby and tumbled out of bed at a little after six the following morning. Oliver was awake in his crib, gurgling and pumping his little legs. Cassie scooped him up and inhaled the scent of lotion and baby shampoo. She never got enough of holding him or cuddling him. She gave him a bottle and when that was done she changed him out of pajamas and into a navy-and-white-striped jumpsuit and popped him in his bouncing rocker, which sat secured by two bolts on the big scrubbed table.

Mouse lingered by the back door waiting to be let out and once the dog was outside Cassie filled the coffeepot.

"Good morning."

Tanner.

She wasn't used to having a man in the house. Doug's visits over the past couple of years had been sporadic. When they were together he was charming and familiar and despite how much she had loved him, didn't set her pulse racing at a galloping speed. Not so his brother. Tanner stood in the doorway, dressed in the same jeans he'd worn the night before and a pale blue T-shirt that enhanced his well-cut arms and broad shoulders.

Once again she was struck by a sense of familiarity... of connection...of memory...of something...

"'Morning," she said chirpily, shaking the feeling off. "Coffee's on and I'm just about to make breakfast."

Oliver chuckled and the sound instantly grabbed Tanner's attention. Cassie watched, fascinated as he made his way toward her son and stopped by the table. Oliver's chuckle became a laugh and she saw Tanner smile. He held out his hand and the baby latched on to his finger. It was both a painful and poignant moment for Cassie. Doug never had the chance to see his son and now Tanner was in her kitchen, making the very connection with Oliver she knew belonged to his brother.

"He's cute," Tanner said and looked at her. "He has your eyes."

"They're brown," she said and poured the coffee. "Like yours."

"The shape is all you, though," he replied. "Lucky kid."

Cassie ignored the fluttering in her belly. Being around Tanner had always done it to her. It didn't mean anything. Just a silly awareness of his good looks. Even a rock would notice.

She started on breakfast and listened as he talked softly to Oliver. He had a nice voice, softly accented and a mix of his Australian roots combined with a quiet, Midwestern drawl. Oliver seemed mesmerized and she had just slid some bread into the toaster when Tanner spoke to her.

"Can I hold him?"

She looked up. "Sure. Do you know how?"

Cassie was sure one brow came up. "I know how. My best friend has three kids," Tanner explained. "He lost his wife in a car wreck when the youngest was a couple of months old."

"That's so sad."

"Yeah, that was two years ago. I help out if I can. Grady owns a place up the road from mine so I'm on hand if he needs a sitter. With three daughters under six he has his hands full."

Cassie watched as he carefully extracted the baby from the rocker. His movements seemed natural and effortless, as if he'd done it a hundred times before. She remembered her own first stumbling weeks when she'd come home from the hospital with a newborn. There were days when she'd never felt more overwhelmed or alone in her life.

Oliver gurgled delightfully and her heart tightened. Tanner cradled the baby in one arm and easily supported his head with a strong hand. "He's a big boy," he said and came toward the countertop. "Clearly a hearty eater?"

Cassie smiled. "He does love his food. He also likes to puke, so watch out."

Tanner laughed and the rumbling sound made her belly flip over. For a reason she couldn't quite define Cassie wished he would stop being so likable. Doug had always been the charming one. So many times he'd said his younger brother was moody and serious with little time for anyone or anything other than his horses and his ranch. The two occasions they'd met she'd had no reason to question that description. He'd hardly spoken to her. Oh, he'd been polite, but there had been almost a cool reserve in his manner. She hadn't taken it personally because Doug had warned her that Tanner wasn't exactly warm and friendly. It had also made the unexpected spark of awareness she'd experienced easier to ignore. But now, watching him hold Oliver with such open affection suddenly seemed at odds with Doug's depiction.

"You're good with him," she said, surprising herself as she buttered the toast.

"Thanks," he replied and tucked the baby into the crook of his arm.

Cassie grabbed a couple of plates and took the food to the table. "He hasn't had a lot of interaction with men. Well, except for Gabe."

His expression narrowed fractionally. "Gabe?"

"My best friend's fiancé. Lauren and Gabe got engaged some months back. They're good friends and very supportive. And Lauren's parents insist I take him to see them once a fortnight. They said he's their honorary grandson, which is nice."

"It's hard when you don't have family."

It didn't sound like a question. And she was quick to remember what he'd said about Oliver being the only real family he had. "Sometimes." She smiled "On the good side there are less birthdays to remember."

He didn't smile back straightaway. "How's your grandfather?"

She was surprised to think he remembered she had any relatives and Cassie quickly explained her grandfather's slide into dementia as she brought fruit and then coffee to the table.

"He doesn't know you at all?"

"Not really," she replied. "Sometimes he calls me by my mother's name. I've taken Oliver to see him a few times but he just sits and looks at us. He's always friendly but I miss the man he used to be. He was all I had after my parents died. He's on dialysis now and has numerous other health issues, including a weak heart."

"I'm sorry."

She shrugged and tried not to let her sudden emotion show. It was difficult talking about her only remaining grandparent. "Don't be. I still like to see him even if he doesn't know me. But I know he's ill and probably not going to be around much longer." She motioned to the food on the table. "You can put Oliver back in the rocker if you like."

"I can manage," he assured her as he pulled out a chair and sat down, positioning her delighted son in the curve of his elbow so he could see her from across the table. He rocked Oliver a little. "I like getting to know my nephew."

"I'd like him to know you, too."

It wasn't the truth. Not really. Because she was confused by her feelings for Tanner. And it was difficult imagining her son could have some kind of worthwhile relationship with a man she hardly knew. A man she wasn't sure *she* wanted to know.

And that, she realized, was at the core of her reticence.

It wasn't about Oliver.

It was the lingering awareness and unwanted attraction she had for Tanner that made her reluctant and suspicious. *They're my own secret demons.* And she had to get over them. For Oliver's sake.

"And your ranch?" she asked, changing the subject. "That's going well?"

He nodded. "Sure. I've mostly been working with injured or traumatized horses for the last couple of years." He managed a wry smile and glanced down at his leg. "Kind of ironic I guess."

She relaxed fractionally. "Doug said you were some kind of horse whisperer."

He laughed and the sound hit her directly between the ribs. "My brother always did like to make me sound like a crackpot."

"I don't think it sounds like that. And you know what

they say—working with kids or animals is one of the hardest jobs in the world."

"I think that's in the movies, Cassie," he said and smiled. "I just train horses to trust people again."

She nodded, thinking that he'd probably managed to accomplish that as easily as he breathed. "And you're happy there?"

He stilled and looked at her. "Yes, very happy."

Cassie swallowed hard. "So you wouldn't...you wouldn't consider..."

"Consider what?" he asked and rubbed a gentle hand over the back of Oliver's head.

She shrugged. "Moving back... Moving here..."

His brows shot up. "To Crystal Point? No. My life isn't here anymore."

She knew that. But unease still rippled through her veins. Because she knew what it meant. "Are you going to sell the house?"

He stared at her with blistering intensity. "Unfortunately, I'll have to."

Her blood stilled. "I could try and raise the money to..." Cassie stopped and thought about what she was suggesting. She'd never be able to commit to such a large debt. Her minimum wage job and the cost of child care put that option out of reach. She shrugged again. "I thought perhaps the insurance might have covered the mortgage."

"No," he said quietly. "There was some other debt and—"

"The Ducati," she said and sighed. "Doug bought it the last time he was home."

"Yes," he said, still quiet. "I'm sorry about the house, Cassie. I know it was your grandfather's home and means a lot to you."

Heat pinged behind her eyes and she blinked quickly.

She didn't want his sympathy. Or his pity. If the house needed to be sold, then she had no option but to go along with his plans. She wanted to ask him about the "other debt," but didn't. What difference did it make now? Her home was going to be sold and there was nothing she could do about it.

"I'll need some time to arrange things," she said and concentrated her gaze on her smiling son. "Perhaps a month to sort through my—"

"There's no rush."

Tanner saw the emotion in her stare. He didn't want to alarm her or make her life complicated. In fact he wanted the opposite. He'd come to Crystal Point to *right* a wrong. To forgive and find a kind of peace so he could get on with the rest of life.

She stared at him over the rim of her mug. *She really does have the most amazing colored eyes.* Eyes easy to get lost in. Eyes that made it even easier to forget that Doug had loved her. And that she had loved his brother.

"I guess that depends on how long it takes to sell," she murmured.

"I have an appointment with Doug's lawyer on Wednesday," he explained. "We'll know more after that."

"We?" She looked skeptical. "The house belongs to you, Tanner. It's your decision. Your call. I've got nothing to do with it."

You've got everything to do with it...

Guilt pressed between his shoulders. And rage toward his brother that he quickly pushed back down. "On paper, perhaps. However," he said and touched Oliver's cheek, "there's more to this situation than an out-of-date last will and testament. And there's little point in imagining the worse outcome before *we* have all the facts."

"But the mortgage—"

"We'll see what happens. And any money left from the insurance will go into trust for Oliver."

"But that's not what Doug wanted," she replied quickly. "He left everything to you."

Tanner knew it had hurt her. How could it not? She was in a relationship with his brother and Doug had failed to provide for her and her child when she needed it the most.

In typical Doug fashion.

It wasn't the first time his brother had betrayed a woman he'd professed to love.

"He would have changed things," Tanner said, lying through his teeth as he looked down at the baby. "If he'd had the opportunity and the time. But he was in a war zone and on a covert mission, Cassie…and probably not thinking clearly."

She sighed heavily. "I know that. He was…surprised… I mean, when I told him about the baby."

Surprised? Tanner knew that wasn't the half of it. Doug had called him at three in the morning in a rage, ranting about how Cassie had deliberately gotten pregnant and probably planned to trap him into a marriage he didn't want. He played devil's advocate as best he could, insisting that Cassie wouldn't be so manipulative. But Doug was unswayed. He didn't want marriage. Or children. And Tanner knew his brother intended telling Cassie as much, had he lived. He had the proof via several emails Doug had sent before he was killed.

The baby gurgled and he grabbed on to the distraction. He couldn't tell her the truth. He wouldn't. It was better she believed Doug wanted to do the right thing by her and his son.

"This little guy is my nephew and I promised Doug

I'd look out for him," he said softly and touched Oliver's head. "And you."

She visibly stiffened. "I don't need looking out for, Tanner. I can take care of myself and Oliver."

The air crackled and Tanner didn't miss the edge of resentment in her voice. Not that he really blamed her. Cassie Duncan had no real reason to trust him. But he didn't want to be at war with her, either.

"Can you at least meet me halfway, Cassie?" he asked. "I know you've been through a lot these past few months, but I'm not your enemy."

"Then what exactly are you, Tanner? My knight in shining armor?"

"How about your friend?" he suggested and the moment the words came out, he felt like a complete fraud. He could never be friends with Cassie. He'd do what he'd returned to Crystal Point to do and then hightail it back home.

She stared at him. "Friends? Sure…"

But she looked as unconvinced about the idea as he was.

He placed Oliver back in the rocker. "I've got a few errands to run. But I'll come back a little later to see this little guy again and get my bags, if that's okay?"

She nodded. "Okay."

Then he left her alone.

His leg ached, and Tanner pressed down heavily on his heel to help ease the pain as he walked from the house and headed for his rental car. He needed to clear his thoughts for a while. And knew just where to do that.

Five minutes later he turned the car into a familiar driveway. The old farmhouse looked much the same, as did the seventy-five-year-old woman who stood on the porch, waving at him to come inside. Tanner waved back and got out of the rental car.

Ruthie Nevelson had lived just out of Crystal Point for

over sixty years. A widow for more than a quarter century, she'd been a friend and neighbor when his folks were alive and a much needed friend to him once they were gone. From her front gate, in the distance Tanner could see the rooftop of the home he'd lived in as a young boy. It was still a working sugarcane farm and he breathed in a heavy, nostalgic breath. If his parents had lived he would have taken over the farm and been the fourth generation McCord to do so. Instead, the place had been sold to another neighboring farmer three months after their deaths and Tanner was shipped off to boarding school a couple of weeks later. After that, he spent the holidays with Ruthie. Doug was in the army by then and returned whenever he could. But there were times when Tanner didn't see his brother for six or more months.

It was Ruthie who showed him kindness and offered comfort and understanding while he grieved the loss of his parents. Not really a grandmother, but as close to one as Tanner had known. It was she who'd pushed him to pursue his talent with horses and arranged the opportunity for him to work with her brother-in-law, a horse breaker and rancher, in South Dakota. After traveling through Europe for a couple of years, Tanner settled in Cedar Creek ten years ago and finally found a place he could call his own.

He locked the car and headed up the path.

"'Bout time you got here," Ruthie said with a wide grin as he took the narrow steps in two strides and landed on the porch. "I've had the coffee ready for half an hour."

Tanner hugged her close. He hadn't seen Ruthie for two years and she still looked as vibrant and healthy as she did back then. Her hair was still dyed an impossibly bright red, and she still wore moleskins, her favorite cowboy boots, and moved with that straight-backed confidence he'd recognize anywhere. Ruthie Nevelson was the best person he'd ever known, and he'd missed her like crazy.

"Hello, Ruthie," he said, smiling broadly. "It's good to see you, too."

She set herself back to get a better look at him. "That leg still ailing you?"

He nodded. "A little. The long flight didn't help. It'll ease up in a couple of days."

"Good," she said and grabbed his arm. "Now, come inside and eat the cake I made for you."

There had always been something about Ruthie's cooking that could cheer him up, and she knew it well. He followed her inside the house and down the narrow hall. Two small dogs came scurrying to greet them and bounced around his feet for attention.

"Ignore them," she said as she dropped her hat on the cluttered counter and pointed to a seat at the table. "They'll lose interest soon enough."

"They're new," he said and pulled out a chair. "What happened to Bluey?" he asked about her old sheepdog.

"Got sick and died last spring," she replied. "Inherited these two when Stan Jarvis passed away a few months ago."

Stan had been Ruthie's on-again, off-again suitor for over twenty years. "I'm sorry to hear that."

She shrugged and grabbed two mugs. "Everybody dies," she said and gave him a wide smile. "Even this old girl will one day."

"Impossible," Tanner said with a grin, then more seriously. "It's so good to see you."

"You, too." Ruthie poured coffee and brought the mugs to the table. "I was expecting you yesterday. Where'd you stay last night?"

"Cassie's," Tanner said as he sat down and spotted a

large frosted cake in the center of the table. He reached out to steal a fingerful of frosting, giving an approving "Mmm" at the delicious flavor.

Ruthie stared at him. "I see."

"It was late when I got there," he explained. "And since I wanted to see the baby anyway, she offered—"

"You told her about the house?" Ruthie asked in her usual straight-to-the-point way.

Tanner shrugged. "We discussed things."

She shook her head. "Messy situation. Typical of that no-good brother of yours."

Ruthie had never pulled punches when it came to Doug. But Tanner respected her too much to disagree. "I'll have to sell the place."

"I thought as much." Ruthie's expression narrowed. "It's not your fault. Some things even *you* can't fix."

Tanner took the mug she offered. "I can try."

She tutted. "And get your heart broke all over again? I dunno if that makes you a fool or a saint."

"I'm no saint," he said with a half grin. "You know that better than anyone."

"What I know is that you can't keep cleaning up his chaos," Ruthie said, her voice harder than usual. "That girl should be told the truth about him."

The truth about Doug? To the outside world he was charming and likable and there was no doubt he'd been a fine soldier. But he'd had troubles, too. In civilian life he'd been unreliable. The army had sorted him out eventually. But it wasn't a truth that Cassie needed to know.

"I'll tell her enough," he said quietly.

Ruthie looked unconvinced. "And will you tell her that Doug McCord got your eighteen-year-old girlfriend pregnant and then dumped her right before he stole your inheritance?"

Chapter Three

No. Tanner had decided. He wouldn't be telling Cassie anything about the girl who'd cheated on him with his brother and when she'd gotten pregnant how Doug had bailed on his responsibility. Or that his brother had taken the money put in trust for Tanner when he reached twenty-one, and used it to fund his partying and gambling. It had ended badly. For him. For Doug. For everyone. But telling tales wasn't his style. And it had been twelve years ago. There was no point in rehashing old betrayals.

"Still protecting him?"

Ruthie's voice got his attention again. "I just don't want anyone to get hurt unnecessarily."

"Anyone?" Her silvery brows came up. "You mean Cassie Duncan?"

"I mean *anyone*," he emphasized.

"She should be told," Ruthie said, relentless. "Putting

him on a pedestal won't change the truth. You were too quick to forgive and forget."

I haven't forgiven.

Not yet. It was why he'd come back. Why he had to make things right for his nephew.

Losing Leah had hurt. Even though their relationship was new and filled with the usual teenage angst, he'd fallen for her quickly. Four months later she'd announced she was pregnant and in love with his brother. But Doug made it clear he didn't want her or the baby and skipped town, taking Tanner's inheritance with him. Unable to get past such a betrayal, it was all the motivation Tanner needed to pack his bags and leave Crystal Point. He spent close to two years backpacking in Europe before Doug finally tracked him down and by then Leah and the baby she'd tragically miscarried were a distant memory to his brother. Doug returned some of the money, said he was sorry, and Tanner did his best to believe him. But the experience had forever changed their relationship. He came home, stayed with Ruthie for a month and then moved to South Dakota.

And he'd never really looked back.

Until now.

Until Cassie.

But he'd already loved one woman who'd preferred his brother. He wasn't about to do that again. No matter how much her blue eyes haunted his dreams.

Still, he was tired of being angry. Tired of resenting Doug and wishing things were different. Tired of living in the past. For years Tanner had battled the anger he'd felt toward his brother. It had kept him shut off and restrained in relationships with almost everyone he knew. Except for Ruthie and his closest friend, Grady Parker, who knew some of what happened between him and his brother.

Almost losing his life in the accident had shifted his

perspective. Tanner didn't want to be angry anymore. He wanted to live the rest of his life without blame and bitterness. And to do that he had to truly forgive Doug. Only then would he find the peace of mind he craved.

"I know what I'm doing," he assured the old woman sitting opposite.

But he was pretty sure she didn't believe it.

She nodded anyway. "So, you gonna stay there tonight?"

"No," he replied. "I'll check into a hotel in Bellandale."

"Nonsense," she huffed. "You'll stay here."

Tanner grinned. "You know, you're getting bossy in your old age."

"Hah…I've always been bossy." Ruthie's throaty laugh made him smile. "Besides, I've got a new colt that needs breaking."

Tanner tapped his leg. "I'm not quite back in the saddle yet."

"No problem. I just need help mouthing and long reining." Ruthie's brows came up and she grinned. "You still look fit enough for that. As long as you can do it without whining like a girl."

Tanner laughed loudly. Ruthie always cheered him up. He left a short time later and headed back to Cassie's. She was in the front yard when he pulled into the driveway. Oliver's stroller was parked nearby in the shade and Mouse sat by the front wheels. She wore cutoff jeans, a gray T-shirt, trainers and thick gardening gloves. A bougainvillea twisted up and across the paling fence and she was cutting off some of the biting vines as he approached.

He patted the dog and flipped his sunglasses off. "Gardening?" He stood by the stroller. "Looks like fun."

Cassie stepped back and turned. "Well, maybe not fun, but necessary at least. I've neglected the yard since Oliver arrived. My grandfather always took such pride in his garden."

Tanner looked around, hands on hips. "It's a big yard. Perhaps getting someone in would be a better—"

She stiffened. "I can do it."

"I'm sure you can do anything you set your mind to." He smiled at the defiance in her expression. "Would you like some help?"

Cassie nodded and bent to collect the gloves. "If you have time. I could make lunch." She stilled and met his gaze. "Unless you've already eaten?"

"No, I haven't."

She held out the gloves. "Great. I'll take Oliver inside and you see if you have any more luck cutting back that vine. See you back in the house in half an hour."

Tanner grabbed the gloves and clippers and got to work on the overgrown vine. He made short work of it and once the branches were hacked he hauled them into a respectable pile. But the spikes, he discovered, were unforgiving and the razor-sharp thorns bit through his T-shirt. He pulled the shirt off, removed the spikes from the fabric and re-dressed before he headed up the path and toward the house.

He cleaned up in the laundry and Cassie was in the kitchen making sandwiches when he rounded the corner and stalled by the threshold. She looked up instantly and brought plates to the table.

Tanner spotted the stroller by the table. "Is he asleep?"

"Yes. I gave him a small bottle and he went out like a light."

Tanner walked into the room and peered into the stroller. Oliver's little face looked peaceful. It occurred to him that he might be able to help out with the baby. "You don't...you know...feed him yourself?"

Her brows came up slowly. "Do I breast-feed, you mean?"

Tanner tried to ignore the ridiculous heat that crawled up his neck. "Yeah."

She shook her head. "I did for a few weeks. But after that I couldn't." She shrugged and walked back to the countertop. "Sometimes it happens that way. I was unwell and after Doug—"

"It's okay, Cassie," Tanner said quickly. "You don't have to explain." No, because he understood. The man she loved was dead, she had a new baby and she was faced with the knowledge that the home she'd lived in most of her life was about to be pulled from under her feet. It wasn't difficult to figure out why she'd struggle to nurse her son.

She shrugged again and he was sure he saw moisture in her eyes before she blinked and turned toward the refrigerator. Half a minute later she returned to the table and sat down.

"Where'd you go this morning?" she asked and pushed a plate toward him.

"Ruthie's," he explained.

She nodded. "Ruthie Nevelson? She sent me a card when Oliver was born. Doug never visited her much. I guess you're closer to her than he was."

"I guess," he said. "I always spent my summers with Ruthie once school was out. Doug was in the army by then."

Cassie looked up and smiled. "My friend Lauren and I used to swipe oranges from her tree when we were kids. Funny," she said and toyed with her sandwich. "We never saw you there. I mean, Crystal Point is a small town— you'd think we would have crossed paths at some point."

We did.

But Tanner didn't say it. Even though the memory was

etched into his mind. At thirteen they'd met briefly. It was fourteen years later that he met her again. And by then she was Doug's girlfriend and hadn't remembered those few moments on the beach so many years earlier.

"I was usually hanging out with my friends," he said, taking a sandwich and smiling. "No time for girls back then."

"And now?" she asked, grinning slightly. "Is there someone in the picture?"

He shrugged one shoulder. "No one at the moment."

"But there was?"

Another shrug. "For a while. It wasn't all that serious."

In truth, Tanner hadn't ever been completely committed in a relationship. For a time, with Ash, he'd thought they might have a future. But it had faded quickly once they realized they were better as friends than lovers. It had ended over a year ago and he hadn't been inclined to pursue anyone since.

"But you want to settle down eventually?"

"Eventually," he replied and took a bite of the sandwich.

"In South Dakota? I mean, you're settled there?"

He nodded. "Cedar Creek is a good town, with good people."

"Like Crystal Point?" she asked.

"There are similarities," he said. "Small towns tend to breed a certain kind of people."

"I suppose they do." She stared into her plate, and then spoke a little wistfully. "Doug didn't share the same beliefs about small-town life. He never seemed happy here."

"It just wasn't his...*fit*," Tanner said. "The military was his home."

She nodded. "Maybe that's why he found it so hard to come back. Even when he did he was always..." She stopped, paused, clearly thinking and not wanting to say too much. "He was always a little unsettled."

Tanner knew that. And knew why. "He wasn't the settle-down type, I guess."

He quickly picked up the way her eyes shadowed. "That's what he used to say about you."

"I mean, he wasn't the type to settle down to a life as a cane farmer."

"I know what you meant," she said, bristling, and pushed the plate forward. "I'm not completely blind to who he was."

There was pain in her words and he gave himself a mental jab. "He did love you," Tanner said and immediately wished he hadn't.

Her eyes lost their luster, as if she was thinking, remembering. "Not enough to come home." She stood and pushed the chair back. "I shouldn't have said that. Doug's gone. Wishing for him to be different is unfair."

"Cassie, I didn't mean to—"

"I need to run a few errands myself this afternoon," she said through a deep breath. "I shouldn't be too long."

Tanner stood and looked at her half-eaten lunch. "I'll finish in the garden while you're gone if you like. And head off when you get back."

"Fine," she said and within seconds had wheeled the stroller from the room.

"What's he like?"

Cassie raised her gaze toward her best friend Lauren and rocked Oliver in her arms.

He's a gorgeous, sexy cowboy who makes my pulse race.

"He seems nice."

Lauren's brows shot up. "*Seems* nice?"

She shrugged again. "What do you want me to say? I hardly know Tanner."

"Apart from what Doug told you?"

True. Only, everything Doug had said about his brother didn't seem to match the man she'd come to know over the past twenty-four hours.

"Okay, maybe he's not the brooding loner Doug made him out to be. Although I'm not going to make too many judgments after one day."

Lauren nodded. "But he wants to be a part of Oliver's life?"

"That's what he said."

"And he's selling the house?"

Cassie drew in a breath. "That's also what he said. There's a large mortgage."

"I'm sorry," Lauren said after a long pause. "I know it isn't what you'd hoped."

"I knew it might come to this," she said, hurting all over at the thought of losing her home, but determined to put on a brave face. "And it's only a house. I'll make a home for Oliver somewhere else."

"You can stay with us," Lauren offered. "You'll always be welcome."

Cassie blinked back the heat in her eyes. "Thanks, but I'll be fine."

"You don't look fine," Lauren said, clearly concerned. "You look pale and tired."

"It's just a headache," she said and managed a smile.

She *did* have a headache. And a scratchy throat and a quickly growing lethargy. But she didn't admit she was feeling increasingly unwell as the day progressed. Lauren's fiancé was a doctor and her friend would have had her under the stethoscope in a heartbeat if Cassie said she was feeling ill.

"If you're sure," Lauren said, still looking concerned. "Just be careful. I don't want to see you get hurt."

Cassie tapped her own chest. "I'm impervious to hurt," she said with a wry grin. "Tough as nails, you know that."

But she knew her friend didn't believe it.

By the time Cassie bundled Oliver into the car and pulled into the driveway it was well past four o'clock. She noticed immediately how the once out-of-control bougainvillea vine was now three piles of tightly bound cuttings and what remained of the hedge had also been carefully clipped back. Plus, the lawn was mowed and the scent of fresh cut grass lingered in the air.

Tanner had been busy. In a matter of hours the front yard was transformed into a neat and tidy copy of what it had once been—before Doug's death, before the bills had piled up and she'd taken leave from her job and had to watch every penny she spent.

Inside, Cassie headed straight for the kitchen and made up formula for Oliver.

She could hear the shower running and once the baby was fed she carried him to the nursery, laid him on the changing table and stripped off his clothes.

"Hey there."

She stilled and turned. Tanner stood in the doorway— hair damp, wearing washed-out jeans and a black collared T-shirt that looked way too good on his broad-shouldered frame. "Hi."

"Did you have a good afternoon?"

Cassie nodded, trying to ignore the throb at her temple. "I went to see my friend Lauren."

"Ah, the orange thief?" he said with a grin.

Cassie laughed softly. "Yes. Were your ears burning?"

He grinned. "Talking about me, eh?"

"Maybe a little," she replied. "I'm going to give Oliver a bath now."

"Sure."

She took the baby into her arms. "Thanks for doing the yard."

"No problem."

Cassie felt the warmth of his stare through to her bones and tried to disregard the heat coiling up her legs. He really did have the sexy thing down pat. She willed some good sense into her limbs and headed from the room, conscious of how he moved aside to let her pass. She lingered in the nursery with Oliver after his bath and by the time she'd dressed him in a navy romper suit and settled him down to sleep it was dusk outside.

When Cassie returned to the kitchen she found Tanner talking to Mouse, and the dog was staring up at him, listening intently. Again, she was struck by the image of the man Doug had told her he was, and the contrasting man he seemed in reality. Not closed off and moody. Not a brooding, unfriendly loner.

Not anything like the man Doug had described.

He looked up. "Is Oliver settled?"

"For the moment," she replied. "He'll sleep for a couple of hours. His usual routine gives me enough time to have a shower and eat something."

Tanner checked his watch. "Then I should probably go."

Something niggled at her. She couldn't define it. Maybe she didn't want to. She drew in a long breath and frowned.

"Are you okay?" he asked, watching her.

Cassie nodded. "I've had one of those daylong headaches."

He laughed and then must have realized how insensitive it sounded. "Sorry, I was thinking that maybe since I've been here for twenty-four hours there was a connection."

She smiled. "No. Although…"

His brows came up. "Although?"

She shrugged. "Well…you're not…"

"I'm not…?"

Heat crept up her neck and she searched for the words. "It's only that you're not exactly who I thought…" She shrugged again and took a deep breath. "I guess I thought you wouldn't be so…easy to get along with."

Tanner rested against the counter and folded his arms. "Compared to what?"

She hesitated as her gaze shifted to the floor. "To the person I thought you were."

"Who you thought I was," he said quietly. "Or who Doug said I was."

Her shoulders came up for a second and then dropped. "I suppose. He said you were quiet and…"

"And what?" Tanner asked when her words trailed. "Indifferent and unfriendly?"

She looked up. "Words to the effect."

"And what do you think?"

Cassie stepped back. "I think you're confident and sensible. I think you don't waste time trying to charm or manipulate people." She paused and took a breath. "I think you know exactly who you are. And what you want."

His brown eyes darkened. "And do you?" he asked softly. "Do you know what you want, Cassie?"

At that moment she wanted to run. Everything about him reached her on some base, heady level. She was hot all over and she knew why. Tanner McCord made her remember she was a woman. And it scared her to death.

"Ah…what about dinner," she said quickly and took a sharp breath. She pointed to the telephone. "I have the number of a great pizza place on speed dial. I mean, unless you want to leave right away."

He pushed himself off the counter. "Dinner would be good."

Cassie nodded and left the room. After checking on Oliver she took only minutes to collect fresh clothes and lock herself in the bathroom. She showered and dressed in cargo pants and a sensible blue shirt buttoned up to her throat.

By the time she headed back to the kitchen another half hour had passed and she ducked her head around the corner of the nursery to ensure the baby was still asleep. At the kitchen doorway she stilled. Tanner stood by the counter, one elbow in the air and he tugged at the back of his shirt.

"Something wrong?" she asked and stepped across the threshold.

He swiveled around and dropped his arm. "I think I caught a barb this afternoon."

"A what?"

"From the vine," he explained and winced.

Cassie walked toward him. "You're hurt?"

He shrugged. "I'll be fine."

"Do you want me to take a look?"

He took a step back. "I don't think so."

Cassie ignored the sudden heat in her cheeks. If he'd been injured pruning the hedge she needed to be sensible and find out how bad it was. "It could get infected."

"I'm sure it will be—"

"Let's see," she said matter-of-factly. "Where is it?"

He hesitated for a moment before moving one shoulder. "Left side."

Cassie stepped closer. "Okay, turn around."

He did as she asked and she took a second before reaching out. His shirt was soft between her fingers and she tugged it down a fraction. When she couldn't see anything other than one incredibly well-defined shoulder blade, Cassie released the shirt.

"It has to come off."

He turned his head. "What?"

"Your shirt," she explained. "I can't see anything. I'm too short."

"I'm sure it's not—"

She ignored him, moved back around the countertop and grabbed the small first-aid kit from the bottom drawer. "It won't take a minute."

He didn't seem convinced and hesitated before he shrugged again and then pulled the shirt over his head and dropped it on the table.

And of course she couldn't look anywhere but at his bare skin.

Sweet heaven.

He didn't possess the body of a man who spent hours in a gym—but of one who worked outdoors, using and honing muscles every day. His tanned skin looked as smooth as the sheerest silk pulled across pressed steel and the light smatter of hair on his chest was incredibly sexy. He was pure beauty and temptation. And she had to stop thinking about it.

"Turn around please."

His eyes darkened and Cassie was sure she caught a tiny smile tugging at the corner of his mouth. So, maybe she did sound way too polite and incredibly tense. That was her nature...her *way*. He turned and Cassie saw where the bougainvillea thorn had pierced his skin directly below his shoulder blade. The spike was easily an inch long and was lodged deep. Cassie opened up the first-aid kit and took out a needle.

"I see it. This is going to hurt," she said. "You might want to brace yourself against the counter."

"Sure," he said and stepped forward, levering his hands on the countertop.

She sterilized the needle and as she moved closer, Cassie tried not to think about his smooth skin and well-defined muscles. Or the fact she picked up the spicy scent of soap and some kind of citrusy shampoo that somehow amplified the awareness she experienced whenever he was near.

With purposeful intent, Cassie reached out and touched him. She sensed rather than felt the tension coiling up his back as her fingertips connected with his skin. She used the needle quickly and started dislodging the thorn.

"Ouch!"

She pulled back. "Don't be such a baby."

He jerked his head around and scowled. "Don't be such a brute."

Cassie stopped the grin that threatened. "I thought you were a tough cowboy."

"I thought you were sweet and gentle."

She sucked in a shallow breath. His words stilled in the air between them. *Sweet and gentle?* Is that how he saw her? Not lonely and guarded and desperate to keep her distance?

"Is that who Doug said I was?"

He didn't respond immediately. "Yeah, of course he did."

Cassie ignored the stab of guilt, grabbed the tweezers and extracted the barb. "All done," she said and stepped back.

Tanner turned and she was faced with the solid wall of chest. She noticed a long faded scar below his rib cage, but other than that there was nothing imperfect about him. Her belly swayed and she got mad with herself. Being attracted to Tanner was out of the question.

Perhaps one day she'd find someone to share her life— a friend, a lover, a husband. Someone who she could love and who would welcome the role as father to her son. But not yet. She wasn't ready. And she certainly had no intention of paying too much attention to the burgeoning attraction she had for the man in front of her.

Still, it was easy to get drawn into the warm depths of his liquid brown eyes. Easier still to stare at his broad shoulders and satin-smooth skin. Heat crept over her skin. *Maybe I have a fever?* Yes, that had to be it. She was unwell. Out of sorts. It had nothing to do with his brown eyes and broad shoulders.

"Cassie?"

His voice brought her stare upward and she locked his gaze as the air flamed, swirling up as it coiled around them. And suddenly she couldn't pretend it was anything other than raw attraction. *Chemistry.* Undeniable and absolutely unwanted.

And from nowhere, a sudden memory kicked in. She'd felt it once before, long ago. She'd all but forgotten that hot summer when she was thirteen. She recalled the boy who'd captured her attention on the beach one late afternoon. Her first crush. Her first kiss. The fluttering in her belly caused a familiar rush and she quickly pushed the memory away.

"I should check Oliver," she said on a shallow breath.

A car pulled out outside.

"Our pizza," Tanner said and grabbed his shirt off the table. "Thanks for the first aid. I'll be back with our dinner."

He walked from the room and Cassie stared after him. Being around Tanner was a mistake. Maybe the biggest of her life.

Chapter Four

Tanner sensed the change in Cassie's mood the moment she returned to the kitchen. He couldn't miss the tension in her expression as they ate and afterward when she refused his offer to help clean up. Uncomfortable by the sudden awkwardness, he left her alone for a while. The awareness between them was hard to deny and he wondered if she realized he was attracted to her and that's why she seemed so closed off. He headed back to the guest room and packed his bag and dropped it in the hallway. Tanner was in the living room looking at the photographs on the mantel when she came into the room some twenty minutes later.

"Everything all right?" he asked and propped the photo of Doug back on the shelf.

"Fine," she replied and pointed to the photograph. "That was taken years ago. I don't have anything current, in case you wanted a copy."

"I have photos," he said and turned. "But thanks."

She nodded. "I also have Doug's things stored away in the spare room. You're welcome to go through the boxes and see if there's anything you'd like to keep."

"Won't you want those as keepsakes for his son?"

"I've selected a few things already. And I have several videos Doug made while he was on tour. Oliver will know his father."

He heard the dig and wondered why she was so tense. It's not as if she owed him any explanations—about anything. "You know, not every conversation we have has to be a battle."

Her eyes flashed brilliantly. "I don't—"

"You act like I'm the enemy."

She crossed her arms and sighed heavily. "Can you blame me?"

He wasn't sure what she was getting at and shrugged. "Which means?"

"I've been in limbo for months, Tanner. Maybe I did shove my head in the sand when it came to the house and Doug's estate, but that doesn't make me any less shocked that you've turned up and now I'm faced with the prospect of leaving the only home I've known since I was a young girl."

Tanner's insides contracted. "I didn't come here to make things harder for you," he assured her. "On the contrary…"

Her brows came up. "Do you think your being here would make things easier?" She shook her head. "The fact is, you're a walking, talking reminder of exactly how much my life is about to change."

Of course he would be. So the sooner he did what he had come to do and then got back to his own life, the better.

"I have no intention of disrupting your life."

"Do I seem so naive to you, Tanner?" She took a couple

of steps farther into the room and seemed to waver on her feet. "Your very presence is a disruption."

She wanted him gone...that was evident enough. "I'm sorry you feel that way, Cassie. Be assured that as soon as I have the estate sorted I'll be returning to South Dakota. But as I said yesterday, Oliver is my nephew, the only family I have, and I'd like to play some role in his life."

"As what?" she asked quietly. "The absent uncle?"

Tanner pushed back the irritation weaving through his blood. Obstinate, infuriating woman. "I'm here now. And I'd like to stay in contact once I go home. It's what Doug would have wanted."

Her brows came up. "Is it?" She paled and an uneasy silence filled the room. When she spoke again her voice was unusually raspy. "Are you sure about that? You and Doug weren't exactly close."

"Things between us improved these last few years."

There was some truth in his words. His brother had tried, in his way, to mend their broken relationship. And Tanner had cautiously let him back into his life. He'd returned to Crystal Point on two occasions to see Doug and his brother had briefly visited his ranch in Cedar Creek six months before his death.

She raised her chin. "He never did tell me why you were estranged."

Tanner's stomach tightened. "It was a misunderstanding that happened years ago."

"Really?" Her brows came up. "What kind of misunderstanding?"

He shrugged. Tanner had no intention of telling her about Leah or the money or anything else from his past. "It doesn't matter now."

She raised her chin in that stiff, determined way he was getting used to. "So you won't tell me?"

"No."

She laughed, the sound brittle in the room. "Well, Doug did say you had a stubborn, unforgiving streak."

He tensed. Of course his brother would have said that. Doug wasn't one to take responsibility for his actions or his *mistakes*.

Her expression narrowed. "What was your relationship like when you were kids?"

"Good," he replied truthfully. "But with twelve years between us we were never really kids together."

She nodded. "You said Doug joined the army at twenty-one and sent you to boarding school?"

"That's right." He named the school that was about two hundred miles west of Bellandale.

"Were you happy there?"

It seemed an odd question. "I've never really thought about it."

She pushed on. "You'd just lost your parents, correct? Why do you think Doug made the decision to send you away when you were so young?"

"He joined the army," Tanner said. "I guess he did what he thought was the best thing at the time."

Cassie didn't look completely convinced. "But what did *you* think?"

He opened his mouth to speak, then clamped it tightly shut. She stared at him, looking intrigued and a little confused. He drew in a slow breath. "I thought… I suppose I thought I'd been abandoned."

"Did you ever tell him that?"

Silence stretched like elastic for a moment. Finally, he spoke. "I don't think I've ever told anyone that."

"Then thank you," she said. "For not dismissing the question. I suppose I'm trying to understand why Doug would have done such a thing. I mean, you really only had each other."

"What twenty-one-year-old wants to be saddled with a kid? Especially someone like…"

Tanner stopped when he saw her expression shift. He met her gaze and waited for her to speak.

"You mean, someone like Doug?" she asked, her voice a bare whisper. When he didn't respond she spoke again. "You know, don't you?"

Tanner shrugged a little. "I know what?"

"You know Doug wasn't exactly thrilled about the idea of having a baby?"

Wasn't exactly thrilled? His brother had flat-out said kids weren't in his plans—ever.

"I know he had some reservations."

She shrugged and maintained her resilient look. "It was a shock, that's all. We'd never talked about children and when I found out I was pregnant I was surprised at first. When I told Doug, he didn't…well, he wasn't happy about it."

He knew the story. Doug had no intention of ever being a father to his child and Tanner knew his brother would have told Cassie that very thing had he lived.

"I'm sure it was the shock, like you said."

As he said the words and tasted the lie, Tanner knew he had to keep the truth from her. It would hurt her deeply if the truth ever came out.

"I suppose we'll never know," she said, softer still.

Tanner shrugged fractionally. "I should get going."

"Are you heading into Bellandale?" she asked.

"No," he replied. "I'm going to crash at Ruthie's for a few days. But I'd like to drop by tomorrow afternoon to see Oliver if that's okay?"

"Of course."

"Good night, Cassie. I'll see myself out."

She nodded and watched him leave. Tanner grabbed his bag from the hall and headed through the front door and realized that leaving was the last thing he wanted to do.

When Cassie sat up in bed at six the next morning she knew the headache and scratchy throat she'd been harboring for days had finally taken hold. But Oliver's cries made her ignore her pains, push back the covers and roll off the mattress. She changed into jeans and a T-shirt, took a couple of aspirin and worked through her sluggishness. It was well past the half hour by the time she'd fed him and then made herself some soothing peppermint tea.

But Oliver was unsettled for most of the morning and in between doing two loads of washing and putting a casserole in the slow cooker, she took him for a long walk. When she got home it was after three and she gave him a bath and a bottle before putting him to bed for a nap.

And even though her head hurt and her throat ached, she kept thinking about what had transpired over the past forty-eight hours. She thought about Doug. And Tanner.

The brothers clearly had a much more complex relationship than she'd realized and Cassie knew that the undivided faith she'd always held in the man she'd loved—the man who had fathered her child—was unexpectedly under threat. Why would Doug have sent a vulnerable and grieving child to a boarding school so far away from the only home he'd ever known? It seemed incredibly callous and at odds with the man she knew. The man she *thought* she knew.

A man she clearly hadn't known.

He'd charmed her with his smile and humor and she'd never really questioned his honesty or integrity.

Until now.

And Tanner? He was very different from the man Doug had described. He wasn't moody and indifferent. In fact, he was the complete opposite. And she was as confused as ever.

With her headache worsening and her whole body slowly succumbing to an unusual lethargy, by four o'clock Cassie grabbed the baby monitor, made tea and then curled up on the sofa in front of the television.

She drifted off to sleep and was plagued by dreams. Of Oliver. Of her parents. Of Doug. And of Tanner. Of his warm brown eyes and sexy smile. When she awoke she discovered a throw had been laid over her bare arms. The monitor was gone from its spot on the coffee table and she sat up quickly. *Oliver.* The headache hadn't abated and she pressed a hand to her temple. It was dark outside and the lamp in the corner gave off a soft glow. Someone was in her house. With the monitor missing, the lamp on and throw draped across her, it was the only explanation. Perhaps Lauren had stopped by? Or M.J.? Both her friends knew where she hid the spare key.

Her legs were heavy as she stood and Cassie rested her knuckles on the side of the sofa for support as she ditched the throw and slipped her shoes back on. She swallowed hard and winced at the stinging pain in her throat. She left the room and headed down the hall toward the nursery. No Oliver. Her heart raced and she rushed down the hallway. And heard voices. Well, one voice. One very familiar, deep and hypnotic voice. She came to a halt in the doorway and listened as Tanner spoke to her son, who he held gently in the crook of one arm while he whisked eggs in a bowl with his free hand.

"—and it won't be a truly superb omelet, of course, without peppers…but it will do. Did you know your daddy was allergic to eggs? I suppose we'll find out if you inherited that from him soon enough. Since you've already had your bottle you might even think about shutting those big eyes of yours and getting some sleep."

"Tanner?"

He stopped talking and whisking and looked toward the door. "Hey there." He turned Oliver around. "Look whose awake, little man. Mommy."

She smiled at her beautiful baby and then looked at the man holding him. "What are you doing here?"

"I said I'd drop by, remember," he reminded her. "And I knocked, around four-thirty. Your door was unlocked."

Cassie felt too unwell to reproach herself for leaving the front door unlocked and then crashing on the sofa. Crystal Point was a safe place…but still…it was irresponsible. Especially with a baby in the house. Although she doubted Mouse would let an intruder in without alerting her. Speaking of which…

"Where's my dog?"

"In the backyard," he explained. "Fed and waiting to be let back in, I'm sure."

Cassie nodded. "You let me sleep."

"You seemed to need it."

She shrugged and tried to ignore the pain in her head. She really was feeling worse with every passing moment. "I guess I did." She looked toward her baby. "He'll need changing before he's put down for the night."

"Done," Tanner said and moved toward her. "I'm somewhat of a dab hand with a diaper these days. I had practice with Grady's kids when they were babies."

Her brows came up. "And you're making dinner?"

"To order," he replied and grinned. "If you don't like omelet."

Cassie thought about her wavering stomach. "Actually, I put a casserole on this afternoon," she said and pointed to the slow cooker on the counter. "But I might just have some soup a little later."

"Soup it is. But first I'll put this little guy to bed."

Normally she would have protested. But the headache and wobble in her knees was getting steadily worse and she didn't quite trust her balance. "That would be great. Thanks."

Once he left the room Cassie sank into a chair and rested her arms on the table. When Tanner returned she was still in that position.

"Everything okay?"

She nodded and sighed heavily. "Just tired I guess. Thank you for watching Oliver."

"My pleasure," he said and came around the table. "He's a good baby. You know, you don't look so great. Are you sure you're all right?"

"I think I'll—"

She stopped as his hand reached out and he rested it against her forehead. "You're burning up."

Cassie's skin tingled from his touch and she pulled away fractionally. "I'm fine."

"You're not fine. You have a fever."

She shook her head and pushed the chair back. "I'll be okay. I only need some rest," she insisted and stood. But her legs wavered and she gripped the edge of the table for support.

"Like hell. You're sick."

And without another word Tanner scooped her up into his arms.

By the time she had the strength to protest he was down the hallway and had shouldered her bedroom door open and placed her gently on the edge of her bed. "Now get some rest."

"You didn't have to pick me up," she protested feebly,

pushing back her embarrassment and trying not to think about how it felt to be held against his broad chest. He was still recovering from an injury and the last thing he needed was to damage his leg again. "I could have walked."

"And fallen over most likely," he said. "You need to take care of yourself, Cassie."

"I will. I *do*. I have a headache, that's all. It'll pass once I get some rest."

"You have a fever," he insisted as he strode toward the bed and pulled the comforter back. "I'll bring you some water. Where do you keep your aspirin?"

She rolled her eyes. "In the pantry, top shelf, but I really think I—"

"Be back in a minute."

She watched him leave the room and then rounded out her shoulders. The man certainly was stubborn. She flipped off her shoes and shimmied farther onto the mattress.

When Tanner returned she pasted on a grateful smile. He passed her a glass of water and a couple of painkillers. "Thank you. I appreciate your concern," she said and looked at him over the rim of the glass. "Even if you are being bossy."

"If it gets you into bed, then I'll do what I have to."

Cassie was sure he didn't mean to sound so suggestive, but once the words were out the air in the room seemed thicker, hotter, as if a seductive wind had blown through the opened doorway. She looked at him, felt the heat rising between them and desperately willed it to go away. But no. It stayed. And grew. And made her mounting awareness of him bloom into a heady, full-blown attraction. *It's because he's handsome and sexy and friendly, that's all.* She'd have to be a rock not to notice, right?

She said his name and waited for several seconds while

he continued to watch her and the heat in Cassie's blood intensified and her cheeks burned. Her skin was on fire and she wondered how much it had to do with her fever, and how much had to do with the man standing beside her bed. She'd never experienced anything quite like it before and despite the headache, sore throat and fever, Cassie knew that whatever she was feeling, he was feeling it, too.

But how? Why? Cassie didn't have any illusions about herself. She wasn't beautiful or glamorous or overly smart. She was pretty at best. The same ordinary girl she'd been all her life. A single mother. *The mother of his brother's child.* The very reason they shouldn't be looking at one another with such scorching desire.

Finally, he spoke. "I should go. Get some rest, Cassie."

"Oliver will—"

"I'll take care of the baby. Just rest."

He left the room quickly and Cassie stared after him. Okay...so they had...*chemistry.*

It didn't have to go anywhere. It wouldn't. It couldn't. She was Oliver's mother. She had a child to think about and fantasizing about a man like Tanner wasn't going to do anyone any good. She dropped back onto the bed and pulled the covers up. Her head hurt, her throat hurt, even her bones ached. Maybe he was right about getting some rest.

I just need to sleep and clear my head.

By tomorrow she'd be over it. And over her attraction for Tanner.

There was no other option.

Around ten the following morning Tanner found Cassie's cell phone and called her friend Lauren. Within an hour she and her doctor fiancé were on the doorstep. Cassie's fever had become progressively worse overnight and by morning she was burning up and clearly unwell. He managed to get her to take some more aspirin and drink a little water just before midnight and she woke again after seven, coughing and shaking from the chills.

"You were right to call us," Lauren said when she came from Cassie's room and met him in the nursery. "Gabe said she has a mild flu. I'll arrange for some medicine to be delivered as soon as possible. That and a few days' rest and she should be fine." She looked at him and smiled. "You don't seem surprised by the diagnosis."

"I'm not," he replied and held Oliver against his chest. He wasn't about to explain he'd spent most of the night alternating between the chair in Cassie's room to make sure he was close by if she needed anything, and the sofa in the living room. If he'd thought it was something more serious than mild influenza he would have bundled her in the car and taken her to hospital. "But I'm pleased she'll be okay."

Lauren gently touched the baby's head. "You stayed last night?"

"Of course."

She nodded slowly. "Well, I'm glad that you're here to look after…things. However, we can take Oliver home with us if you—"

"No," he said quickly. "That's not necessary. I'll stay until Cassie's feeling better. And I'm sure she'd prefer that Oliver remain here."

He thought she might insist, but Lauren only nodded. "You're probably right. Let me know if you need anything. You have my number."

They left a few minutes later and Tanner quickly checked on a restlessly sleeping Cassie before he headed for the kitchen to feed Oliver. He'd become quickly attached to the little guy and was enjoying the time he got to spend with his nephew. Oliver was a placid baby and caring for him made Tanner think about the prospect of having children of his own. One day. He was surprised how much he liked the idea. The ranch could be a lonely place and more so than ever before, he let himself imagine a couple of kids running across the yard to the house and then along the wide verandah. And a woman…a wife. Someone to talk to. Someone with soft skin and warm hands to curl up with at night. Tanner liked that idea, too.

He'd spent so many years pouring all his energy in his horses, building the ranch and trying to live in the present and forget the past he'd somehow ignored the future. But being with Cassie made him think about it.

No, he corrected immediately. It was Oliver who got him thinking. Cassie was just… She was just the girl who'd sparked his interest all those years ago on the beach. Being around her brought back those memories, that's all. He had a handle on his attraction for her. And he'd forget all about it once he went home.

Only, last night he could have sworn he saw something in her eyes…a look…a connection…and it was something he hadn't expected. Because she'd loved Doug.

Which means she can never be mine.

He shook the feeling off. The less he thought about Cassie being his or anyone else's, the better. Tanner put the baby down for a nap and then took a quick shower. He dressed back into his jeans and padded barefoot down the hall toward the spare room. He rummaged around and found some of Doug's clothes hanging in the wardrobe. He pulled out a shirt and slipped it on. It was a little tight in the shoulders and baggy around the waist, but it would do. He stayed in the room for a while and flipped through a few of the boxes. He found his brother's uniforms neatly packed inside one box and another smaller carton held his medals. Tanner sat for a while, looking at the collection of memories. What would Doug make of him being with Cassie and Oliver? Would his brother be angry? Resentful? Would he eventually have come around to the idea of being a father to Oliver?

Tanner didn't think so. Doug liked his freedom. Strange, then, that he'd joined the military. But Tanner understood why. His brother needed the army to give him companionship. And to give him solitude. Within the corridors of discipline and routine he found the family he'd needed. He'd bonded with people who understood him, who were like him, who had his back. Tanner knew his brother had never felt that with his real family. When their parents were killed Doug was already estranged from them. He'd never fit into the life on the farm. He'd never wanted to work the sugarcane and small herd of cattle. Doug had bailed at eighteen and headed for the city, where he worked a succession of transient jobs. After their parents' accident he returned and reclaimed what he believed was his...and promptly sold off Tanner's legacy.

Then came Tanner's years at boarding school. During that time he learned to despise his brother...and yet still love him. He was family. And family was everything. Despite the repeated betrayals. Despite Doug's behavior with Leah. Despite the mishandled inheritance. Despite all of it, a part of him still wanted to believe in the idea of brotherhood.

Tanner ignored the heavy feeling in his chest, folded the box shut and got to his feet. He headed to the kitchen, heated up some soup he found in the pantry and carried a tray into Cassie's room.

She was sleeping and he was pleased that the racking cough that had kept her awake for most of the morning had abated for a while. Tanner slipped the tray onto the bedside table and watched her for a moment. She stirred and let out a soft moan. The soft hum of the humidifier he'd found in the nursery cupboard and set up by the bed was the only other sound in the room. He noticed she'd pushed the blanket aside and moved closer to pull the cover back up. She looked peaceful in sleep and as he watched her a strange sensation knocked behind his ribs. For years he'd put her out of his thoughts and programmed himself to *not* think of her. But when Doug died that changed. He had a blood tie and a responsibility to Oliver. His nephew would never feel what he had when he was a child—alone, abandoned, discarded. He'd always be there for his brother's son regardless of where he was or what he was doing. Oliver was his only family and family was all that mattered.

And Cassie?

She was Oliver's mother and that was all she could ever be.

She'd loved Doug. Wanted Doug. Borne his child. Which meant she was off-limits. Despite how being around her messed with his head, his libido and his heart. His attraction to Cassie would fade once he returned to South Dakota and got back to his regular life. He'd put her from his mind before. He could do it again.

One thing he knew for sure…he wasn't about to fall in love with her.

Not a chance.

Chapter Five

When Cassie awoke it was dark outside. She knew she'd been drifting in and out from sleep and wakefulness for several hours. Or was it days? Her head and throat still hurt but she sensed the fever that had taken hold so quickly had mostly left her body.

She pushed back the covers and eased herself into a sitting position. The bedside lamp was on and she heard the gentle hum of the humidifier from somewhere in the room. The digital clock read 6:45 p.m. but she had no idea what day it was. She looked down and noticed the cotton pajamas she wore. They were pale lemon and had silly-looking cats on them. Cassie didn't remember changing her clothes. Didn't remember much of anything, really. Only a deep voice that had given her an easy comfort as she'd shifted in and out of sleep, and then someone pressing a glass to her lips so she could have some water. Then she remembered another voice, female and familiar. Lauren.

Her friend had been looking after her. Of course, it could only have been Lauren.

Cassie swung her legs off the bed. The house was quiet. Too quiet.

Oliver...

Where was her baby? Panic crept over her skin for a second, and then she realized he must be with her friend. Cassie forced herself to stand, and when her knees wobbled she clutched the bed to get her bearings. Once she had her balance she grabbed her robe from the foot of the bed and pushed her arms into it and tightened the belt. She made a quick bathroom stop and then moved back into the bedroom. The door was open and she made her way across the room as steadily as she could. A light illuminated down the hall and she followed it to the nursery. But the room was empty. The panic returned and quickly seeped deep into her bones. Where were they?

She turned on her bare heels and hurried back down the hall to the kitchen.

Still nothing.

When she reached the living room Cassie came to an abrupt halt in the doorway as relief flooded every pore. Oliver was safe. But he wasn't with her friend. He was lying blissfully asleep against his uncle's strong chest.

Tanner was in the recliner, legs stretched out and crossed at the ankles, both hands cradling her sleeping son. He wore jeans and a white tank shirt and his feet were bare. His eyes were closed and his hair flopped over his forehead a little.

Cassie's belly rolled over as she watched them. In a matter of days she'd witnessed him form a bond with her son that touched her to her very core. It was the bond she'd dreamed Doug would have had with his son. But it wasn't

Doug cradling her child so gently. It wasn't Doug who'd been so kind to her over the past few days.

Doug was gone.

And Tanner was now in her life. Until he left. Until the house sold and Doug's estate was sorted. She needed to remember that he was passing through. He was temporary. And once he was gone her life could return to normal. She'd find somewhere to live, go back to work and raise her son…and forget all about Tanner McCord and his sexy smile and broad shoulders.

She looked at him again. His eyes were now open and he was smiling.

"Hey there," he said softly. "How are you feeling?"

Cassie nodded. Her arms were aching to hold her son, but the thought she might be contagious stopped her from rushing forward. And Oliver looked so peaceful and content resting against Tanner's chest.

"Okay," she replied and stepped a little farther into the room. "Weak. I guess I've been out of it since yesterday?"

"Pretty much," he said and pushed up from the chair effortlessly. Oliver didn't protest, but instead seemed to snuggle closer to his uncle. "He was restless," Tanner explained and gently touched the baby's head. "And he seems to like this."

She smiled warmly. "Thank you for taking care of him."

Tanner met her gaze. "That's what family is for, Cassie."

Her throat tightened. *Family.* It had been so long since she'd thought she had anyone to call family. With her grandfather's slide into dementia and Doug's continued absence from her life even though she'd considered them a couple, Cassie had felt very alone for the past few years. Oliver's arrival had changed that of course, but he was a baby and needed her 24/7. To have someone to rely upon, to *need* someone herself, was a different kind of feeling.

Not that she *needed* Tanner. Not at all. But he'd said they were family…and for the moment, while she was feeling so weak and weary, it made her feel a little less alone.

"How about I put him in his crib and then make you some herbal tea?" Tanner suggested quietly.

Cassie nodded. "That would be good."

Careful not to wake the baby, he slowly got out of the chair and came to stand beside her. Cassie's heart rolled over when she gazed into the face of her sleeping son and she touched Oliver's head gently. Glancing up, she saw Tanner watching her with a kind of blistering intensity and the look made her insides quiver. His eyes were dark and hypnotic and she was quickly drawn into his stare. So close, with only Oliver between them, she was more conscious of him than she had ever been of any man in her life. There was a connection between them…a link that had developed over the past few days. And it wasn't simply about Oliver.

This was something else.

This was physical attraction…pure and simple.

An attraction she'd always been able to ignore. Until now.

"Be back in a minute," Tanner said, breaking the visual connection.

He left the room and Cassie let out a long breath. There was nothing right or reasonable about her feelings. Nothing she could say to herself that would assuage the heaviness in her heart. He was Doug's brother so desiring Tanner was out of the question.

He returned about ten minutes later and Cassie was sitting on the sofa, legs curled up, her chin resting in one hand. He came into the room with a tray and placed it on the small table beside the sofa.

"I heated some soup," he explained and passed her a mug. "You should probably eat something."

Cassie took the mug of warm broth and smiled. "Thank you. You've been very kind."

He shrugged loosely, as though he was embarrassed by her words. "It's nothing."

That wasn't even halfway to the truth. She managed a wry smile. "Ah...how did I get into these pajamas?"

"Lauren," he explained. "She was here this morning."

Cassie nodded a little. "Oh, I don't remember much of today."

"Her fiancé checked you out and she organized the medication you needed. She also suggested taking Oliver home with her for the night, but I thought you'd prefer he stay here."

"I do," she said quickly, hating the idea of being apart from her baby. "And you stayed?"

He shrugged again. "It seemed like the right thing to do. You were in no condition to look after Oliver last night and today."

She was tempted to thank him again but sensed it wasn't what he wanted to hear. Instead she sipped the broth and settled back into the sofa. It was strange, she mused, how comfortable she was being around him. She hadn't expected it. On the two occasions they'd met before she'd always had her guard up, and always felt as though Tanner had, too. But this time was different. There was no one to hide behind. No one to whisper words about how unfriendly and indifferent he was. No one to tell her he was the kind of man who preferred his own company and his horses to having real relationships. Cassie was seeing him without Doug's bias and prejudice for the first time... and she liked him. A lot.

"So, I guess you should stay tonight, too?"

The intense way he was watching her made it impossible to look anywhere but into his eyes.

"Do you want me to stay?"

Cassie took a second and then nodded. "I think Oliver would like it."

So would I...

"All right," he said and watched her over the rim of his coffee mug. "I'll return to Ruthie's tomorrow."

"Thank you."

Silence stretched between them and Cassie waited for discomfiture to crawl across her skin. When it didn't come she knew it was because she'd quickly become accustomed to Tanner's company. Despite how attracted she was to him and despite how much she knew it could never go anywhere, he was easy to be around.

He was, she realized, nothing like the man Doug had so often described.

Instead of being a moody closed-off loner, he was friendly and generous and considerate. And he possessed a laid-back kind of charm she found increasingly difficult to overlook. In the kitchen, the garden or the nursery he did everything with such an easygoing confidence it was impossible to *not* be attracted to him.

Admit it...you're also thinking he'd be good in the bedroom...

Cassie shook the thought away. It was stupid. She still loved Doug. And she was a single mother. A soon-to-be homeless single mother who didn't have time to waste thinking about Tanner in that way. In any way, for that matter. But it had been such a long time since she'd thought about strong arms and a broad chest. And longer still since she'd thought about sex. With anyone.

"Are you sure you're feeling okay now?" he asked softly.

"Positive," she lied and managed a smile. "Soup and

sleep therapy will work a treat tonight and I will be back to my usual self by tomorrow."

He nodded. "It's getting late... You shouldn't wear yourself out."

She was touched by his concern. But a part of her wondered if he wanted to shuffle her off to bed so they wouldn't be alone. He had to know she was attracted to him. And she was pretty sure it was mutual. He obviously thought it a bad idea. Which of course it was.

"So, what are your plans?" she asked. "I mean, once you've finishing saving the day here?"

He grinned. "I didn't realize that's what I'd been doing."

"Sure you did," she said and smiled a little.

He shrugged again. "I have an appointment with Doug's lawyer on Wednesday. After that I'm not sure. We'll have to see what the lawyer says."

We...

As if it was inclusive. As if it had something to do with her. As if...well, almost as if they were a couple.

Cassie silently cursed her foolishness and ignored the flush rising over her collarbones at the thought of the idea. Two days together didn't make them anything. "I know you said there was no hurry for me to start looking for a new place to live, but I can't see the sense in putting it off. I could never afford to take on the mortgage here, so the sooner I accept the inevitable, the better."

Tanner's insides contracted. He hated hearing the disappointment and pain in her voice. This was her home. The home she'd made for her son. The home she'd known as a young girl when she'd moved in with her grandfather after her parents had been killed. It had to hurt her. He knew only too well what it was to lose the one place that had made him feel safe when he was a child. He wanted to make it right. But nothing he said would offer her consolation or comfort.

"Like I said, we'll wait and see what the lawyer has to say."

She shrugged as though it didn't matter, but Tanner knew she was resigned to losing her home. And once again he silently cursed his brother. Doug should have provided for Cassie and his son. He should have ensured they had a place to live and were financially secure.

"I think I'll get some rest," she murmured as she placed the mug down and stood. "Thank you again for everything you've done for Oliver…and for me. I know this probably isn't what you expected to be doing when you made the decision to return to Crystal Point. I'm very grateful for your concern and kindness."

Tanner stared at her and a heavy sensation uncurled in his chest. She had a way of doing that to him. It made him feel weak…almost vulnerable. And it gave her a power over him he was certain she didn't know she possessed.

"Good night, Cassie," he said and got to his feet. "Let me know if you need anything."

What I need is a cold shower…

Even in her silly pajamas and nightgown, with her hair mussed and slippers on her feet, she was beautiful and sexy and warmed his blood. No other woman had ever had quite the same effect on his libido. Sure, he'd dated several women over the years…but Cassie Duncan stirred him like no one else ever had. He'd fought it for years, convincing himself that she loved his brother and his own feelings were of little consequence. But sometimes, like the way her blue eyes watched him when she thought he wasn't looking, Tanner couldn't help wondering if she regarded him as more than Doug's brother. More than Oliver's uncle.

Don't be an ass.

Of course it was stupid. And wrong. She'd borne his brother's child. She was clearly still in love with Doug. She'd made it clear that she didn't really want him in her life.

So get moving and take that cold shower.

"Good night," he said again, firmer this time so he could galvanize himself into action and get away from her. "I'll lock up."

She nodded and left the room. Once he was alone Tanner let out a long breath, flicked off the lights and waited until he heard her bedroom door close before he walked from the room and checked that all the windows and doors were locked around the house. Once he was done he moved down the hallway and headed for the bathroom. He took a shower and turned in around nine, spending the next couple of hours staring at the ceiling in between getting up to check on Oliver. By midnight he'd had enough. He pulled on jeans and a shirt and made his way to the kitchen.

A soft glow illuminated down the hall and when he rounded the doorway he noticed the light above the stovetop was on. Cassie was sitting at the kitchen table, a mug cradled between her hands. She'd changed into gray sweats and her hair was pulled back in a ponytail.

"Hey," he said easily, despite the inexplicable tightness that filled his chest. "Couldn't sleep?"

She shook her head. "No. You?"

Tanner nodded and remained in the doorway. "Lingering jet lag, I guess."

"And with looking after Oliver you haven't exactly had a chance to sleep it off, right?"

He shrugged. "It'll work itself out. You, on the other hand, should be resting."

"I think I've slept enough for both of us," she said through a brittle smile. "I had a shower to freshen up and didn't feel tired, so I thought I'd have some green tea and sit for a while," she said and sighed. "I was thinking about Doug."

Of course she was. Tanner didn't doubt that his brother was on her mind most days and nights. "Then I'll leave you—"

"Do you know the details about what happened?" she asked unexpectedly, cutting him off.

Tanner stilled. "Details?"

"About the incident."

"You mean how he was killed?" he queried.

She nodded. "You're his official next of kin so I figured you had the details. I know he was on some covert mission and that he and two other members of his squad were killed by a sniper...but that's all I know. Since I wasn't listed as family it's been almost impossible to get information. I know you got the army to forward his belongings here, but did you know this house wasn't even listed as his place of residence? Instead it's some post office box I didn't know existed and don't even have a key for. And there's a safety deposit box, too, did you know that? I don't have access to it, of course. But I'm guessing you will."

Tanner didn't respond. He didn't want to say anything about the safety deposit box until he'd had a chance to go through the contents himself. He certainly hadn't suspected that Cassie knew about it. Doug's lawyer had told him about it along with the details of his will.

"I'll see what I can find out," he said vaguely. "There's also the matter of Doug's military pension. I'm sure there'll be some money available for you and—"

She waved a hand and frowned. "I don't want any kind of handout," she said and cut him off again. "And I intend to go back to work when my maternity leave is up."

"And Oliver?" Tanner asked as he walked behind the

kitchen counter and grabbed a mug. "What are your plans for him?"

"Day care," she said. "Which is the option of most working single mothers. There's a good day care center not far from the hospital where I work."

"But if there's money available you could—"

"No," she said, interrupting him once again. "Doug obviously wanted his estate to go to you. I can't and won't challenge his wishes."

Tanner wasn't sure whether she was being altruistic or just foolishly naive. "It's not that simple."

"Yes," she defied. "It is."

He flicked on one of the lights and then rested his hands on the counter. "Oliver is Doug's son. Which makes him the beneficiary of my brother's estate. And also the recipient of any benefit that may come about from the years Doug spent defending this country. I won't argue, Cassie. Not on this issue. You can look at me with those beautiful, big, blue eyes all you want…but I won't change my mind on this."

She stilled suddenly, watching him as a tiny half smile creased the corner of her mouth. "You think I have beautiful eyes?"

Damn…

Tanner ignored the way his heart thundered in his chest and shrugged as casually as he could. "Well, I'm not blind." He stopped, thinking he shouldn't say anything else. But good sense *didn't* prevail. "And you're very…pretty."

She laughed softly and raised both brows. "I've always thought I was kind of average."

Tanner frowned. *Average?* There was nothing average about Cassandra Duncan. "You're not serious?"

"Perfectly," she replied. "Doug said I—"

"Doug was an ass."

She laughed again and the delicate sound echoed around the room. "Really?"

"I meant that he—"

"He did have some *ass-like* qualities I suppose," she said and grinned. "But then, no one is perfect, right?"

Except for you...

Tanner pulled himself back from saying anything stupid. Or rather, something even more stupid. "I shouldn't have said that."

"Are you referring to criticizing Doug or complimenting me?"

Was she being deliberately provocative? Tanner couldn't tell. He knew so little about her. Her moods, her thoughts... they were a mystery to him and he knew it needed to stay that way. "Both."

She sipped the tea and then placed the mug on the table. "Well, what's a little harmless flirting? It doesn't—"

"Is that what we're doing?" he asked quickly, fighting the heat climbing over his skin.

She gave a brittle laugh. "I'm not sure what we're doing. I'm not sure what *you're* doing."

Going slowly out of my mind...that's what.

Tanner straightened. "You know why I'm here."

"I know what you came here to do," she said quietly. "I'm still not sure why."

"Does it matter?" he asked, reluctant to say too much. "For Oliver, like I said."

"And to sort out Doug's estate," she added, watching him closely, as if she was looking for answers in his expression. "When we both know you could have done that through lawyers. The house needs to be sold. There's no money left to speak of other than a possible military pension. So if this is all about Oliver, if my son is the real reason you've come all this way, I want to know why. I want to know why family is so important to you, when it didn't seem to matter one way or another when Doug was alive."

There was strength in her voice and a kind of unexpected determination to get answers. She was annoyed. And she wasn't hiding it.

"Okay," he said on a long breath. "The truth is, I don't want Oliver to feel…abandoned."

Her gaze sharpened. "Like you were, you mean?"

"Exactly."

She nodded a little. "But Oliver has me. He's not alone. And I'm not about to shuffle him off to boarding school when he's of age. And although I do appreciate that you want to have a relationship with your nephew, Tanner, I can't see how it will be sustainable once you're back in South Dakota. A part of me is reluctant to let him get attached to you when I know you'll be leaving soon. I know he's only a baby, but he's already bonded with you and I—"

"I intend to come back and see him when I can," Tanner explained, hating all her relentless logic.

Her brows came up. "Like you saw Doug? Once every couple of years? Tell me, how often did Doug visit you when you were at boarding school?"

"Not often."

She shrugged. "I can't see this being any different."

"I'm not Doug," Tanner said. "And if his son—my nephew—ever needs me, then I'll be there."

She looked into her mug for a moment and then lifted her gaze. "It's a nice idea and I guess only time will tell. But have you considered what will happen when you get married and have a family of your own?" Her eyes were questioning. "You do plan to do that, don't you?"

His insides burned. "At some point."

"Do you really think you'll have the time or inclination to nurture a relationship with Oliver when that happens?"

"I won't abandon him."

"You can't take Doug's place in his life."

Tanner gripped the counter. "It hadn't occurred to me to try."

Her brows came up again. "Are you sure? You seem to have ridden in on your proverbial white horse. I'm not saying that I'm not…grateful. I am. Especially with being sick these past couple of days. But it's not your job to look after us. And frankly, I don't want to take advantage of your…generosity."

"You're not," he assured her. "I'm here because I want to be here. I mean, with Oliver. I made a promise and I intend to stick to it. Doug would want me to make sure his son was provided for."

It wasn't exactly the truth. Since Doug hadn't any plans to claim the child he'd fathered or the woman who'd loved him.

She inhaled heavily. "I hardly saw him, you know… I mean, in the last twelve months before he was killed. He returned for about a week, but he was restless…like he didn't want to be here. Like he was waiting to get back to his other life." She shrugged. "That was the week Oliver was conceived. And it was the last time I saw Doug."

Tanner remembered that visit. Doug had called him, complaining about how Cassie was pushing for commitment and how he wanted out of the relationship. He'd talked his brother out of doing something rash, but three months later Doug called again…and this time he wasn't going to be swayed. Cassie was pregnant. He didn't want commitment. He didn't want fatherhood. He didn't want to be tied down to a life he wasn't suited for. Tragically, by paying the ultimate sacrifice for his country, his brother had gotten the freedom he'd craved.

Tanner wanted to tell her that Doug *would* have come

home to claim his family. He wanted to tell her that she would have had the happy-ever-after she deserved. But he couldn't. Because it wasn't anywhere near the truth. Doug had been a fine soldier, but in his personal life he'd repeatedly left wreckage in his wake.

"I'm sorry it didn't turn out the way you were hoping it would."

She gave a derisive laugh. "He told you, I suppose, that I had brought up the subject of marriage."

Tanner nodded. "Yes."

"He said we'd talk about it when he got back. Only, he never did get back. And we never talked."

"Some people just aren't the marrying kind, I guess."

Her eyes widened. "So you don't think he would have married me and settled down?"

Realizing he might have said too much, Tanner backpedaled. "It doesn't really matter what I think."

"But Doug talked to you," she persisted. "And he obviously told you how he felt about the baby coming."

"He was surprised," Tanner said too casually. "And in a war zone. I don't imagine he had the chance to absorb much of anything at the time."

"I suppose. I only wish… I wish that he'd met Oliver… that he'd had a chance to know this perfectly beautiful baby and hold him just once. I'm sure if he had he would have…he would have felt like I do."

Tanner wasn't so sure. But he didn't say anything. Because her blue eyes were now glistening brightly and her tremulous voice echoed around the room. She dropped her face into her hands for a moment and sighed heavily. Seeing her sudden anguish, he walked around the counter and moved closer. She looked up to meet his gaze and within seconds there were tears on her cheeks.

Without a word he sat down and reached for her hands,

taking them gently within his own. She didn't protest. She didn't move. The only sound in the room was the faint tick from the clock on the wall and the gentle hum of the refrigerator. And she wept. Not racking, uncontrolled sobs, but quietly, with restraint and a calm kind of dignity.

As he held her hands and felt the connection of her skin against his own, a tide of long-buried feelings rose up and hit him squarely in the solar plexus. He pushed them back, willing them away with all his strength because he knew they were futile.

"I'm sorry... I don't know what's come over me," she said, still crying.

Tanner squeezed her fingers gently. "You're tired, you've been ill *and* you're grieving, Cassie. Don't be so hard on yourself."

Tears trailed down her cheeks and he fought the impulse to wipe them away. He wanted to take her in his arms and console her. But he wouldn't.

"The more time that goes by, the less I feel I knew him," she said shakily. "It's like there's this wall of disconnect that keeps getter wider with each day that passes. Sometimes I'm afraid that I'll forget what he was like and I won't be able to tell Oliver about his father."

"That won't happen," Tanner assured her and gently rubbed her fingers. "We both knew Doug... We can both tell his son the kind of man he was. How he was brave and fought for his country. How he could make people laugh with his lame jokes. How, even when we were mad as hell with him, we couldn't help loving him."

She nodded and looked at their hands. Still linked. Still connected. And making his heart beat faster with each passing second. He met her gaze and sucked in a sharp breath when he noticed her lips part fractionally. He knew it was an unintentional invitation, but it was an invitation all the same and the very notion of her lips against his made his skin burn.

He wanted to kiss her. Just as he had all those years ago. He wanted to hold her, as he'd imagined countless times since.

But this was Cassie…the woman who'd borne his brother's child. She'd loved Doug. Just like Leah. And he wasn't about to let his heart get smashed.

Not ever again.

No matter how much he was tempted.

Chapter Six

Cassie was captivated. There was something about the way Tanner looked at her that defied logic. Defied good sense. Defied every warning bell in her head telling her she was crazy to be so achingly aware of him. His brown eyes searched her face, lingering on her mouth, and there was enough heat in his gaze to combust the air in the room. Something rattled around inside her head. A sense. A feeling. It was both familiar and breathtakingly new. She wondered how he could do that to her. How, even though they barely knew one another, there was a growing energy between them that drew her toward him in a way she hadn't expected. *If* she believed in past lives, *if* she believed that two people could have a connection that belied the depth of their acquaintance, she would have sworn they'd somehow shared a moment of time together.

The feeling lingered and she couldn't have moved if she'd tried. She looked to where his fingers stroked her hand and felt the heat of his touch through to her very core. He had nice hands, big and tanned and just a little calloused on the tips. Hands that were made for schooling the most skittish colt, but hands she'd seen soothe her baby son to sleep as no others had. Cowboy's hands, she mused, forged from hard work and skill.

Her thoughts shifted and she wondered how it would feel if his fingers traveled slightly up her arm. The quiet intimacy of the room amplified her awareness of him and Cassie let out a long, shuddering sigh. He felt it, too; she was sure of it. The intensity in his gaze couldn't be faked and the tenderness of his touch was wholly mesmerizing.

It had been so long since she felt a connection to someone.

And the fact that someone was Tanner McCord scared her to pieces.

He drew her hand to his mouth and softly kissed her knuckles. It should have sent her running. It should have had her jumping up in protest and demanding an explanation. But she didn't move. She didn't break the contact.

He did.

Tanner released her hand and got to his feet, staring at her for a few long seconds. "Good night, Cassie."

By the time he'd left the room she was shaking all over. By the time she finally tumbled into bed ten minutes later she was certain she had to pull herself together.

And fast.

It was past seven when she rolled out of bed the next morning. Tanner was in the kitchen preparing Oliver's bottle and she barely looked in his direction when she entered the room and made a beeline for her baby, who was happily chuckling away in his bouncer. It felt so good to hold her son after a day without having him in her arms.

She took a deep breath and inhaled the sweet baby smell that always gave her such comfort.

"Good morning."

Finally she looked at Tanner. He'd pushed a steaming mug of coffee across the counter and Cassie half smiled. "Ah, thanks."

"This is ready to go," he said and shook the bottle in his hand a little. "You want to feed him?"

"Oh, yes," she replied and moved toward the counter. She took the bottle and quickly settled herself at the table. Oliver latched on immediately and she relaxed when he began to feed.

"You're feeling better this morning?"

She glanced up. Tanner hadn't moved from his spot behind the counter. "Yes, much."

He nodded. "Good. Then I'll get going."

"Tanner, I think—"

"I'll call you after my meeting with the lawyer."

There was a terseness to his voice she hadn't heard before. The easy friendship they'd developed over the past few days seemed to have disappeared. He clearly wanted to leave and she had no intention of stopping him. "Okay, sure."

"Goodbye."

She nodded a little. "Yeah...goodbye."

Then he was gone from the room and Cassie barely drew another steady breath until she heard the front door close and the faint sound of his car pulling out from the driveway.

By the time she'd fed and bathed Oliver it was close to nine o'clock, and after she put him down for a nap Cassie took a shower, tied up her hair, applied a little makeup and changed into jeans and a pale lemon-colored sweater.

Keeping busy stopped her from thinking about Tanner, which was exactly what she wanted.

At ten she'd had an unexpected visitor—her longtime friend Mary-Jayne Preston.

"You're here?" Cassie said once they'd finished hugging in the doorway. "I thought you were neck-deep in orders and holed up in your workshop?"

Her friend shrugged. "I bailed and came to see you instead."

Cassie grinned. "I'm so glad you did. But do you want to tell me why?"

Mary-Jayne, or M.J. as she was affectionately called, tossed her mane of dark curly hair. "Not especially. Today was merely just another boring event in my mundane life."

There was nothing boring or mundane about Mary-Jayne Preston. Her beautiful and talented friend designed jewelry. She was vivacious, fiery and had strong ideals about politics and the environment.

"You're the most *un-boring* person I know," Cassie said and ushered her guest down the hall.

M.J. grinned. "I think I'm just restless."

Cassie raised a brow. "Are you thinking of taking off again?"

M.J. often went on spur-of-the-moment vacations to obscure places. Cassie had always envied her friend's fearlessness and adventurous spirit and sometimes wished she was a little more like her. She'd never traveled. She'd never even been on an airplane. Doug had complained many times that she'd lacked daring and was too set in her ways. She always shrugged it off, but deep down she was hurt by his words.

"Maybe," M.J. replied and sat at the table. "You know how I feel about being trapped by routine. But enough about me... How are you doing?"

"I'm good," she fibbed and smiled.

"Lauren said you've been ill," M.J. said, suddenly serious. "Do you need me to do anything for you? Perhaps help out with Oliver?"

She shook her head. "No, I'm fine. I've had—"

"Help?" M.J. asked with a grin. "Yes, so Lauren told me. I hear a certain cowboy has been here."

"Tanner," Cassie explained, and ignored the heat in her cheeks. "Yes…that's right."

"Is he still gorgeous?"

Cassie allowed herself to smile fractionally. "Oh, yeah."

"Does he still make your knees go weak?"

Cassie colored hotly. "I've never said he does that."

M.J. laughed softly. "Maybe not in so many words."

"You're incorrigible." She grinned. "But the truth is…"

"Yes?" M.J. prompted.

"He's…nice. Much nicer than…"

"Much nicer than Doug ever said he was?" her friend asked bluntly when Cassie's words trailed off.

"I guess so. I mean, I knew they didn't have the closest relationship…but there are things Doug said about Tanner that now seem so far from the truth."

M.J.'s brows rose sharply. "You mean Doug lied?"

She nodded. "I suppose he did. It's almost as though he wanted me to think badly of his brother."

"Perhaps so he could make himself look like the better man?" M.J. suggested.

Cassie's mouth flattened. The idea of that sounded mean and spiteful. It wasn't how she wanted to remember the man who'd fathered her child. "I know you think I was blind to Doug's faults, but I did know he wasn't perfect."

"He never deserved your love, Cassie," M.J. said quietly. "Or your loyalty. The way he reacted when you told him you were pregnant was truly awful. You know that in your heart."

Cassie did know it. And Mary-Jayne, with her tell-it-like-it-is personality, was only saying what Cassie knew herself deep down.

"He would have come around to the idea of being a father," she said, way more animated than she felt. "With time, things would have been better." She sighed and looked at her friend. "I have to believe that. For Oliver's sake."

"I get what you're saying," her friend said gently.

But she knew M.J. didn't really understand. And she didn't want to explain any further. If she didn't remain loyal to Doug's memory, then she'd be forced to question her reasons for loving him. Without that love to hide behind she'd be vulnerable...and with Tanner McCord in town, being vulnerable was out of the question.

When Tanner arrived on Cassie's doorstep on Wednesday afternoon he didn't expect to be greeted by a stunning-looking brunette with wide green eyes, who regarded him with a kind of guarded curiosity.

He stepped back on the porch and forced out a smile. "Is Cassie home?"

The brunette leaned against the door frame and shook her head. "So, you must be *the jerk's* little brother?"

Okay. Now he knew who she was. Doug had told him about Cassie's friend who had always been a very vocal critic of his brother's continued absence from Cassie's life.

"Tanner," he said, ignoring the jerk taunt. "You must be M.J. Doug mentioned you once or twice. Nice to meet you."

M.J. grinned. "I'm watching the baby while Cassie's

out visiting her grandfather. She should be home around four. You can stay and wait if you like."

He glanced at his watch and then politely declined her offer. "Just tell her I stopped by and I'll call her later."

Knowing that Cassie was visiting her grandfather made him think about his own family. And the visit he'd been putting off. Tanner got back in the rental car and took the fifteen-minute drive to the cemetery where his entire family was buried. His parents' dual headstone greeted him as it had so many times in the past. He stared at their names, forcing memories into his head. So much about them had been forgotten. But the feel of his mother's embrace and the deep comfort of his father's voice remained locked inside. So many years had passed. Over two decades of being without them and it struck him how similar his story was to Cassie's. They'd both lost their parents around the same time. His died in a car wreck, hers in a boating accident. Thankfully she'd found a home with her grandfather, which he hoped had lessened her loss just a little.

He took a deep breath and turned his gaze to the right. Doug's headstone was glaringly white beside the faded one of their parents. Tanner's stomach churned and emotion quickly thickened his throat as he read the words.

Douglas Ian McCord. Aged 41. Son. Brother. Soldier. Killed in action. Never forgotten.

He blinked away the heat in his eyes. In that moment the loss of his brother hit home in a way it hadn't since the moment he'd heard Doug had been killed. Tanner pressed a palm to his chest to ease the sharp jab of pain that knocked him with the force of a runaway train.

He experienced a mix of emotions. Hate and love. Betrayal and forgiveness. Relief and anguish. Over the years he'd felt them all in one way or another when it came to his brother. After Leah had told him she was in love with Doug and carrying his brother's child, Tanner had shut down and vowed to never speak to the other man again. At eighteen, his heart had been fueled with rage by the knowledge of Doug's treachery. His inheritance was gone. The girl he'd loved was gone. He'd packed his bags and taken off for Europe, never intending to look back.

Two years had passed before Doug tracked him down and for so long afterward Tanner wondered why his brother had sought him out. For a man who didn't want commitment or anything or anyone tying him down, he'd worked hard to rekindle their broken relationship.

Guilt...

He hated to think that was his brother's sole motivation. But nothing he'd done later in his life made Tanner believe that Doug had changed. Not when he'd bought a house he clearly couldn't afford or wasted money on cars and bikes he'd never use. Not when he'd secured the love of another woman who would go on to bear his son, and then have every intention of casting them aside.

No...his brother hadn't changed.

But he *still* grieved the loss of his only sibling. And he still wanted him back so he could tell him what a damned irresponsible fool he was.

"Tanner?"

A soft voice said his name and he turned. Cassie stood by his parents' headstone, her hands clasped together. In her kitchen he'd almost kissed her beautiful mouth. And he was certain she wouldn't have stopped him. Which meant one thing.

Complicated.

He stepped back, leaning heavily on his uninjured leg

and moved beside her. "I thought I'd come and pay my respects," he said quietly.

She nodded. "I usually stop by on my way back from seeing my grandfather."

"How is he?"

"Granddad?" She stepped closer. "He's had a bad week and didn't know me today."

Tanner saw the pain in her expression. "That must be difficult."

She shrugged. "Yeah…but he's eighty-two and has lived a full life. Not like…"

"Like Doug?" he queried when he noticed her gaze flick to the headstones. "Or my parents? Or your parents?"

"Yes, exactly." She pointed south. "They're down that way."

"Shall we visit?"

She frowned a little and looked at Doug's grave. "You don't want to stay here?"

"I've said my goodbyes."

She lingered for a second and then nodded and, as she turned, the scent of her perfume caught on the breeze. It didn't take long to reach the spot where her parents were and Tanner hung back while she stood at the foot of their graves. She remained there for barely a minute and then turned back to him.

"I've had enough now," she said and started moving away.

"It's hard for you to be here?" he queried as they walked down the path.

She shrugged. "I guess I don't want this place to be how I remember them. No one's life is defined by their headstone."

"You're right," he said and moved in step with her. When they reached their vehicles and she'd flicked the lock mechanism on her sedan he opened her driver's door. "If it's okay with you I'll see you back at the house. I went to the lawyer today and there are some things we need to discuss."

Her small smile faded. "My friend Mary-Jayne is at home looking after Oliver and she always stays for dinner on Wednesday night, so now is probably not a great time."

"I met her," Tanner said and grinned. "I dropped in earlier. Colorful girl."

Her smile returned. "She's a straight shooter. And she never liked Doug much, if that's what you mean."

"She didn't call him anything he didn't deserve," he said drily. "So, how about you play hooky for an hour so we can talk?"

She frowned a little, but then pulled her phone from her bag. "I'll call M.J. and say I'm going to be late. Where would you like to go? Perhaps Ruthie's? Or we could go to the beach and sit on one of the tables near the kiosk."

"The beach," he answered quickly, thinking he didn't want to talk to Cassie beneath Ruthie Nevelson's interested eyes. "We can grab coffee from the kiosk if you like."

"Ah...okay. See you there."

The Crystal Point beach was an idyllic spot where the Bellan River met the sea. There was a surf club near the holiday park and a kiosk that catered to the locals and tourists. It was off-season, so the park was mostly vacant and the kiosk quiet. Tanner parked outside and waited for Cassie to pull up beside him. He got out, locked the car and met her by her door.

Five minutes later he'd bought take-out coffee and they were making their way along the path that led to the beach. They stopped before they reached the sand and took a seat at a concrete picnic table.

"So," she said, getting straight to the point, "what did the lawyer say?"

Tanner took a steady breath. "He confirmed what we already knew. There's a mortgage and some credit card debt. The insurance covered some of the debt but there's still a sizable amount owing."

She wrapped her hands around the foam cup. "And you have to sell the house?"

"Yes."

Her breath came out heavy. "Well, that's not exactly unexpected. I'll start seriously looking for a new place tomorrow."

"It's not that urgent," he said and watched her over the rim of his cup. "The house needs some work done to it before it goes on the market if we're to get the best price."

She sighed. "I know I've let it run down since—"

"It's not your fault. Nor was it *your* responsibility. But I don't want to keep going on about what Doug *should* have done. I'll fix the house up and hopefully it will sell quickly. Whatever money is left from the sale will go into trust for Oliver."

She returned the barest nod and met his gaze. "Will… will I need to get DNA testing done to prove Oliver is Doug's child?"

"You're not serious?"

Color rose in her cheeks. "I thought you might want proof before you handed any money over."

"No," Tanner said gently. "I know whose child he is, Cassie. He has Doug's eyes."

"And yours," she said.

"A family trait," he said and smiled. "He's a beautiful child and I'm glad I've been able to get to know him."

"I'm glad, too." She cradled the cup in her hands. "I know I've been a bit hot and cold about you being part of his life…but I am genuinely pleased that he has an uncle who cares about us."

* * *

She hadn't meant to say "us." But the word slipped out and it was impossible to avoid the query in his gaze. He did care; that was obvious. He was a caring, kind man and she'd been naively deceived by Doug into thinking Tanner was some sort of closed-off, unfriendly loner who didn't need or want any kind of familial relationships. He did want them... The way he'd bonded so effortlessly with Oliver was evidence of that.

"I'll help you get the house ready," she said and smiled. "Some of the rooms need painting and the backyard could do with an overhaul. And perhaps some new light fittings. It shouldn't take long to fix up."

"Sure," he replied. "And don't stress about moving. When the time comes we'll find a place for you both."

"And what about the safety deposit box?" she asked. "Did you find anything important in it?"

He shook his head. "No. It was empty."

It seemed odd, but Cassie didn't press the issue. She nodded and finished her coffee. "I think I'd like to walk for a while."

"Want some company?"

Did she? Being around him was increasingly unsettling. And since the tense moment in the kitchen when he'd comforted her she'd done little else but think about him. She could have sworn he was going to kiss her...and not just on the hand as he'd done. Naive and inexperienced she might be, but there was heat between them and spending time with him only added fuel to the fire.

She should have sent him on his way. *Should have.*

"Okay," she said and got to her feet.

He stood and tossed their empty cups in the trash. "Lead the way."

The beach was deserted and when they reached the

sand she flipped off her sandals and shoved them into her tote. There were gray clouds rolling in from the sea and the wind whipped up around them. "I love it here on days like this," she admitted as they started walking along the sand. "It's got a mysterious mood about it when the clouds rumble and the wind howls."

He laughed. "Cold wind and unswimmable seas...not exactly my idea of a great afternoon at the beach."

"Wimp," she said and laughed back. "Where's your sense of adventure?"

They walked closely together and Tanner quickly steadied her when she lost her footing and tripped.

"Oh, sorry," she said breathlessly, gripping his arm. "I'm something of a klutz."

"I bet you're not. Doug told me you were a dancer when you were young."

She grimaced. "Not exactly. I did ballet with Lauren when I was about ten. But I lasted only a few months."

"Best I not take you to the upcoming Rosemount Rodeo, then," he said and grinned. "There's a cowboy dance being held in the evening. Don't want you stepping on my feet."

She released his arm. "I saw flyers advertising the rodeo when I was in town the other day. It's about half an hour out of Bellandale, isn't it?"

"About that."

She nodded a little. "I've never been to a cowboy dance. I'm not sure I'd know how to move."

"It's easy. You just hang on to one another and sway."

Suddenly the notion of hanging on to him, be it dancing or otherwise, sent another surge of heat coursing through her veins. It had been so long since she felt a man's arms around her. And she missed it. She missed intimacy and closeness and...sex.

Not that she'd had much of a sex life in the past few

years. Doug's visits were so infrequent and brief before she'd fallen pregnant with Oliver she'd begun to question his commitment to her and their relationship. Being involved with a career soldier was one thing…being involved with a man who could leave so easily time and time again, another thing altogether. Doug wasn't tied to Crystal Point. And there were times when she'd wondered if she was little more than a cook and housekeeper for him to come back to every now and then. She'd also wondered what might have happened if Oliver hadn't come along. She knew in her heart there would have to have been some serious changes to the dynamic of their relationship if it was to last.

It certainly wasn't the relationship she'd dreamed of when she was younger. As a teen she'd had her share of romantic fantasies. She'd been quiet and studious and anything she knew about romance and love she'd learned through novels and old movies.

Well, almost everything…

Once, long ago, she'd been swept off her feet. By a boy riding a horse, no less.

She'd been on the beach with Lauren and they'd spotted the lone rider at the edge of the river mouth. Horses were common enough on the beach, so she hadn't taken much notice, until her thirteen-year-old eyes had realized the rider was a boy around her age, and that he looked too gorgeous for words in jeans, plaid shirt and cowboy hat resting low over his eyes. Lauren had pushed her forward when he'd come close and she'd tentatively said hello. He'd done the same and they'd chatted for a couple of minutes. He was on vacation, staying with a relative. She'd explained she lived in the small town permanently. It had been puppy love at first sight for Cassie and she'd agreed to return the following afternoon and he was already riding off on his horse when she'd realized they hadn't exchanged names.

"What are you thinking about?"

She glanced sideways when she realized Tanner was looking at her. "Nothing. You'll think it's silly."

"Try me," he said with a wry grin. "Sometimes we all need a little silly in our lives."

Gosh, he was *so* right. She was tired of being serious all the time. Of worrying. Of overthinking. Of being a grown-up. Some days she longed to be frivolous and just have *fun*.

"All right," she said and took a deep breath. "I was thinking about how right over there," she said and pointed to a crest of sand covered in clumps of grass, "is where I got my very first kiss."

His gaze narrowed. "Really?"

"Yep. I was thirteen and very naive." She laughed and grinned. "Hard to imagine, huh?"

He smiled, as though he'd guessed she was a teenage dork. "And?"

"And he was a boy I met on the beach. He was a cowboy," she said and met his eyes. "Like you, I guess. He had a horse and a hat and a nice smile and he kissed me."

"And that's it?"

She shrugged. "It was enough. It was everything a girl's first kiss should be… It was sweet and soft and his lips tasted like peppermint."

She smiled coyly, embarrassed by how foolish she must seem to him. But Tanner wasn't laughing. He was watching her with such burning intensity she couldn't move. The wind whipped around them and she shivered even though she wasn't cold. Something kindled between them. A look. A memory. Something she couldn't fathom. For the thousandth time she wished she knew him better. And she wished she wasn't scared to death of letting him into her life and then knowing he'd be out of it once he left.

"Anyway," she said, stepping back. "It was a long time ago. And I never saw him again."

"So he just kissed you and took off?" he inquired, continuing to walk. "That's not exactly chivalrous."

Cassie took a few long strides to catch up with him. "Actually, *I* took off. I spooked and ran." She came to a sudden stop and waited for him to halt and turn around. "We should get back. I promised Mary-Jayne I wouldn't be too long."

He crossed his arms, unmoving. "So why did you spook and run?"

"Because that's what I do," she admitted on hollow breath. "When it comes to getting close to someone I guess I spook easily."

He stared at her. "You didn't run from Doug."

"He was never around," she said quickly, hearing her words echo on the breeze. *Did I really say that?*

"But you wanted commitment," he reminded her. "Marriage, family…right?"

"I thought so," she said warily, feeling the intensity of his gaze so acutely it was like a fire racing over her skin. "But maybe…"

"Maybe it was safe to want it from Doug because you knew you'd never get it?"

There was something so elementally powerful about his words she stepped back, stunned by how much truth she heard. Was it possible? Had she set her sights and her dreams on a man she knew would never be able to deliver? Were her expectations and hopes that low?

"I don't know. Perhaps," she murmured, wavering between a sudden rage at Tanner for working her out, and an irrational fear that no one else ever would. "I don't usually psychoanalyze myself."

"You mean you don't dwell on your abandonment issues?"

"I don't have—"

"Sure you do," he said gently. "You lost your parents at a vulnerable age and now you expect everyone else to leave you, too."

"You lost your parents around the same age and you don't have—"

"Of course I do," he said, sounding suddenly impatient as he cut her off. "Anyone who loved Doug ended up as collateral damage in one way or another. I know that from experience. He dumped me into boarding school, remember? Why the hell do you think I'm back here, Cassie? Why do you think it's so important to me that Oliver doesn't grow up thinking that the people who are supposed to protect him didn't bail and take what's rightfully his?"

Chapter Seven

The moment the words were out of his mouth Tanner wanted to snatch them back. He'd said too much. Revealed too much. *Felt too much.* Cassie's eyes were wide and filled with questions. And he couldn't and wouldn't say anything more.

"What does that mean?"

He shook his head and turned. "Nothing. Let's go back."

"No," she said firmly. "I want to know what you mean. We're talking about you, not Oliver. We're talking about something Doug did to you…something he took from *you*. What was it?"

"Nothing," he said again and started walking back toward the kiosk.

Cassie moved up beside him and grasped his arm. "Tanner, stop. I want to know. I *need* to know."

"You don't need to know this," he replied and brushed her hand away.

"Please," she implored. "Tell me. Stop treating me like I'm made of glass. I can handle it...whatever it is."

"Go home, Cassie," Tanner said flatly. "I'll call you about the house in a day or so."

He strode up the beach and waited by their cars until she caught up. When she reached him her cheeks were ablaze and her blue eyes bore into his like icy chips.

"You're a real jerk, McCord, you know that!"

He bit back a grin. She had spunk, that's for sure. And he'd rather see her spirit than her tears. "Talk to you soon."

"So, that's it? You're just going to leave?"

He opened the car door. "I won't be far away."

That didn't seem to give her any comfort. "Go to hell."

He grinned. "Well, I'm not going that far...but I'll be at Ruthie's if you need me."

With that, she gave him one last glare before she got in her car and drove off.

By the time Tanner returned to the Nevelson farm it was past five. He hit the shower, changed into jeans and a T-shirt, and joined Ruthie on the porch for a beer.

"Girl trouble?" she asked with a wide grin.

Tanner bit back a smile. "Don't know what you're talking about."

Ruthie didn't let him off the hook. "You've got the look of a man with a woman on his mind."

He did, but he had no intention of admitting it. "I've got no such thing," he said and drank some beer.

The older woman harrumphed. "Deny it all you like, but I know what I see. Call me sentimental, but I don't wanna see you get hurt."

"I won't," he said quietly. "I know what I'm doing."

Yeah...right.

Ruthie didn't look convinced. "Just make sure you do.

And don't forget you promised to start long reining that ornery new colt tomorrow."

He hadn't forgotten. In fact, he was looking forward to working with the animal. It had been over a week since he'd been near a horse and he missed it as he missed air in his lungs. Plus, he knew working with the colt would take his mind off Doug, Cassie and the letters he'd discovered were in the safety deposit box that afternoon. Letters from Doug. Letters written on old-fashioned paper and with the gold fountain pen that had belonged to their grandfather. Letters to him. To Cassie. Letters his brother had written and sent because he was going into a covert, dangerous mission and wasn't sure if he'd return. They were essentially words written by a man who had predicted his own death. As expected, his brother had begged his forgiveness one final time while insisting none of his past actions were done out of malice. Tanner wanted to believe it. They were Doug's last words to him and should have given closure, and might have if it weren't for the letter he'd written to Cassie. It wasn't sealed and Doug would have to have known he'd read it. Tanner was also sure his brother would know he'd never let her read the words that would break her heart. Perhaps that's what Doug was hoping for? Maybe his brother wanted him to let him off the hook. And he would. But not to protect Doug. Rather to protect a woman who deserved better. Because it was there, in black and white, every possible callous, unfeeling thing a man could say to the woman who was going to have his child. As Tanner had scanned the pages, all the suppressed rage and censure he'd felt toward his brother had risen to the surface and consumed him like a rogue wave.

And he knew one thing.

Cassie would never know the truth.

His brother's legacy wouldn't be that of an unscrupulous

and self-absorbed bastard who didn't care who he hurt. She could spend her life thinking of Doug fondly and without knowing he intended to abandon her and the child she'd borne. Just as he'd done with Leah.

He'd give Cassie a few days to cool off and start work on the house the following week. But he missed Oliver. And he missed her, too, as much as he knew it was foolhardy. He had enough on his mind without wasting time missing her. The house had to be sold and hopefully it would go to contract before he headed back to South Dakota. He'd spoken to a couple of real estate brokers earlier that day and was sure the property would sell quickly once it was painted and the yard tidied up.

As promised, Tanner spent most of the next day long reining Ruthie's colt. He didn't hear from Cassie and figured she was still mad at him for shutting down their conversation at the beach. But he'd said too much. Besides which, he'd been sideswiped by her admitting she'd been kissed there for the first time.

He remembered everything about that day. He'd come to stay at Ruthie's for a couple of weeks during summer vacation and spent most of his time working his horse. When his parents died, Ruthie had agree to keep Rusty, the buckskin gelding he'd owned since he was a small child, at her farm. Vacation time was always spent at the Nevelson farm. That morning he'd been working Rusty along the sand bed. It was low tide and he'd spotted a pair of teenage girls watching him from the crest of a small dune. Boarding at a boys' school meant limited interaction with girls, and naturally curious about the opposite sex, he'd headed across the sand. He'd pulled up in front of the dune and heard their combined giggles.

The girl with pale blue eyes had immediately captured his attention and when she'd smiled Tanner's insides had jumped all over the place. They'd talked for just a moment and then Tanner had dipped his hat lower, clicked Rusty into a trot and headed back over the dune. But with the promise to meet her again the following day.

That's when he'd kissed her. Her first kiss. His, too.

Fourteen years later he met her again. Only this time she was living in Doug's house and sharing his brother's bed. And she didn't remember him. There was no recollection in her eyes. He'd been forgotten. As had their kiss.

Or so he thought.

But he had no intention of telling her that he was the boy she'd kissed. Things were complicated enough already. And he had enough on his mind without dwelling on that teenage kiss.

On Saturday morning, however, she turned up.

Tanner was in the corral and he eased the colt to a smooth halt when he saw her car pull up outside the farmhouse. He watched as Ruthie came down the steps and greeted Cassie by the vehicle. The two women chatted for a moment, and then Cassie pulled Oliver from the backseat. Within seconds the baby was in Ruthie's arms and he heard both women laughing. Something uncurled in his abdomen as he watched them together. Cassie's laughter traveled across the yard and he tried to concentrate on the horse and forget her. Which was impossible. Because while Ruthie took Oliver inside the house, Cassie headed toward the corral. And to him.

She really had no idea what she was doing. Except that she wanted some answers. And fast. She'd been stewing for three days. Getter madder, more confused and more determined than ever to find out what Tanner was really playing at. By the time she reached the round yard she was short on patience and breath.

He stopped what he was doing when she reached the fence.

"Cassie…hello."

He wore dark jeans and a blue shirt that stretched across his shoulders and outlined the strong musculature of his chest. His sleeves were rolled up and he wore a wide-brimmed cowboy hat. He looked, in a word, gorgeous. And he'd been in her thoughts all week.

"We need to talk."

He smiled. Damn. There was a tiny dimple in his cheek. How had she never noticed that before?

His brown eyes caught her gaze. "What about?"

"You know very well," she snapped back. "I may seem like a gullible doormat to you, Tanner, but be assured that I am not."

He actually laughed. "Doormat? I don't think that."

"You must," she said, hands on hips. "Otherwise you wouldn't keep avoiding my questions like a coward."

That got him. Right where it hurt. Because he was out of the corral and barely two feet in front of her within seconds. And he was angry. Well…good. She was angry, too. He stared at her. Through her. And with such blistering intensity it made her knees weak.

"So…go ahead," he said, his jaw so tight his lips barely moved. "Ask me."

She swallowed hard and ignored the rapid thump of her heart. "What happened?" When he didn't respond she pushed further. "What did Doug do?"

Tanner's expression was like granite. "There's no going back from this, Cassie."

"I don't care."

"Okay. Don't say I didn't warn you." He took a breath. Sharp. Short. And then he spoke. "He stole my inheritance."

Cassie stepped back. "What? I don't know what that means?"

"When our parents were killed he sold the farm that had been in our family for five generations and then shuffled me off to boarding school. The proceeds were split and since Doug was my legal guardian he had access to my trust fund."

"How...how much money was there?"

He named the sum. A huge amount. Hundreds and hundreds of thousands.

"And he stole it from you?" she asked, horrified. "From his only family?"

Tanner nodded. "Yes. He gambled. He wasted it on questionable investments. He bought cars, boats...anything he wanted."

"But why would he do—"

"Because he was selfish and irresponsible," he said, cutting her off. "Because he was like two different men. He was the soldier, brave and trustworthy. And he was the civilian, self-absorbed and deceitful." Tanner took a long breath. "Are you happy now, Cassie? Does knowing what Doug was capable of give you some insight you didn't previously have?"

She didn't want to believe it. Didn't want to imagine that the man she thought she loved could do something so despicable. "That's why you hated him."

He shook his head. "I didn't hate him. He was my brother and I loved him. I just didn't like him very much. And I made a promise to myself years ago that I would never act like him. Never be that kind of man."

Cassie sucked in some air. She had her answer. "That's why he left everything to you. He was ashamed."

"Probably."

"And that's also why you don't want the house and why

you're so determined not to challenge the terms of the will. And why you want to leave any money in trust for Oliver. Right?"

He nodded. "Right."

Cassie felt sick to the stomach. "I can't believe he'd do such a terrible thing."

"I've no reason to lie to you."

"I know that," she replied. "And I believe you. I just don't want to believe it."

"I told you there was no going back from this."

The sour taste in her mouth remained. It was reprehensible. The lowest of acts. And she was glad she knew.

"You know, despite what you think, I've never worn rose-colored glasses when it came to Doug."

One dark brow came up. "Really? You seemed to put up with his behavior for long enough."

"What does that mean?"

He shrugged one magnificent shoulder. "You said yourself that Doug was never around. Who puts up with that? Who values themselves so little that they would settle for a man who appeared to just want a warm body in his bed whenever he was in town?"

His words cut her to the quick, and without thinking she slapped his face. It was the first time she'd ever done anything like it.

Mortified, Cassie stumbled backward and landed against the fence. Her hand stung and she could see the growing outline of her fingertips on his cheek. Shame washed over her and she drew in a shaky breath. "I'm so... sorry... I shouldn't have—"

"No," he said with a wry half smile as he rubbed his cheek. "But I probably deserved it."

She wanted to agree, but couldn't. There was no excuse for what she'd done. "I really am sorry, Tanner. I don't know what it is about you…but you push my buttons in a way that's very confusing. One minute we're friendly and the next there's this…this unbelievable tension that I can't explain. But I am sorry I hit you. I would certainly never condone violence in any—"

He laughed loudly and she stopped speaking. "Ah, Cassie…I think we're both…*tense*. And I think we both know why."

There was an intimate, seductive tone to his voice and it wound up her spine like liquid. Cassie pushed back further against the corral and drew in a shallow breath. "I don't know what—"

"Sure you do," Tanner said as he stepped closer and rested one hand on the top fence rung. "And it certainly hasn't been easy being attracted to you and not being able to do anything about it."

Oh, sweet heaven…

Cassie's legs turned to Jell-O. She swallowed hard, watching him observe the movement of her throat with scorching intensity. He was close and she could feel the heat emanating from his body. Desire thrummed between them and she couldn't have denied it if she'd tried. It had been building all week. And longer. Since the first time he'd come to visit Doug several years earlier. Being around Tanner had made her nervous, on edge. Back then she'd put it down to him being unfriendly and distant. But now she knew the truth. He wasn't unfriendly. He was funny and charming and personable. The distance she'd felt had been of her own making. Her nerves were fueled by her awareness of him. Of her attraction. And now she had nothing to hide behind.

He wanted her.

She wanted him.

It was as simple—and as complicated—as that.

He reached up and touched her hair, twirling a few strands between his fingertips. The heat grew. Her awareness amplified by his close proximity. She could have ducked beneath his arm and ran. She could have found safety in the house with Ruthie and Oliver and defied the sudden desire racing across her skin.

It's wrong to want him…

But she didn't move. Every part of her was attuned to Tanner in that moment. Her breasts were barely inches from his chest and she fought the urge to press closer, to feel his strong body, to run her hands down his shoulders and arms and lose herself in his kiss.

"Do you think I'd do it here?" His voice was little more than a husky whisper as he looked down into her upturned face. "Do you think I'd kiss you here…out in the open? Is that what you want?"

What she wanted was to drag him into the stable and tear off his clothes and make love with him. Mindless, hot sex that would satisfy the passionate hunger thrashing through her body.

"No…no…" she said, her denials trailing off as he moved a little closer.

There was almost nothing between them now. Barely a whisper of space.

"You're sure?" he queried, his mouth against her ear.

Cassie felt his warm breath and her skin quickly turned to gooseflesh. No man had ever had such a profound sexual effect on her. Not Doug. Nor the one lover she'd had before him. This kind of thing didn't happen to her. She was an ordinary woman having an extraordinary reaction to the most beautiful man on the planet. And she couldn't control it. Couldn't contain it. Couldn't do anything other than stare into his dark brown eyes and wonder what his kiss would taste like, what his touch and complete possession would feel like.

And again, as if it had happened countless times before, she experienced a jolt of hazy recognition way down deep. As if…as if she'd known his kiss…his touch, in some long forgotten memory. In another life. Another time.

"We should get back to the house," he said softly, unmoving.

He was right. Ruthie Nevelson would have a bird's-eye view of them from her house. She was probably up there wondering what they were up to. They weren't touching. Weren't kissing. But she was pretty sure that from a distance it looked exactly as if they were.

"Yes," she said finally and ducked past him. "Good idea."

Her legs were still wobbly, but by the time she walked across the yard and reached the porch steps she'd regathered her composure and had stopped visibly shaking. She tapped on the door and waited for Ruthie's invitation to enter. She'd never been inside the Nevelson farmhouse before. But it was big and filled with beautiful antique furnishings. Cassie followed the sound of the other woman's voice and found her in the kitchen, with Oliver bouncing happily in her lap.

"He's an adorable little boy," Ruthie said when Cassie entered the room. "I can see why Tanner is so smitten."

Ruthie's brows were both up, as though there was a question in her words. Cassie did her best to ignore it. Imagining Tanner *smitten* or anything else wasn't good for her peace of mind. And it confirmed her suspicions that Ruthie had seen them by the corral.

"He's a good baby," she said as casually as she could. "I feel very blessed."

"You should," Ruthie said and sighed. "Every child is

a blessing. I never got to have any myself. But there's no point wailing about what isn't to be. Life's too short for wailing, don't you think?"

Cassie smiled. There was something incredibly likable about Ruthie Nevelson. It didn't surprise her that Tanner was so fond of the older woman.

Tanner...

In between the *almost kiss* and learning about what Doug had done, she was more confused than ever. Thinking about Doug's betrayal was mind-numbing. That he could be so callous, so inconsiderate and deceptive, chilled her to the bone. She felt deceived, too. By the man she'd believed she knew. By the man she'd believed she loved. Tanner had suggested she was simply warming Doug's bed. Was that all she was to him? Had she put her blinkers on to avoid seeing that was *all* she was?

As hard as it was to admit, Cassie knew that a man who could steal from his younger brother in such a terrible way could easily fool a gullible and trusting woman into thinking he loved her.

"Yes," she said and laughed softly. "There's no point in wailing. No point at all."

They heard a sound coming from the back and Ruthie got to her feet. "That'll be Tanner. Got him working to keep his mind off things."

"Things?" Cassie echoed.

"You know," Ruthie said and grinned. *"Things."*

You...

That's what the older woman meant. And Cassie wished she could work to take her mind off him, Doug and everything else. Not even Oliver could keep her thoughts on track.

"You know he's a good man, don't you?" Ruthie asked unexpectedly.

Cassie's skin heated. "Yes, of course I—"

"Too good to be messed with," Ruthie said and looked toward the back door. "You know what I mean. He got his heart broke a long time ago... I'd hate to see that happen again."

Cassie stilled. Obviously Ruthie was referring to what Doug had done with his inheritance. And of course Tanner was hurt by his brother's betrayal.

"I don't see how it will," she said and took Oliver into her arms. "He's leaving in a few weeks and won't be back for a while. If ever."

Ruthie looked at the baby. "Oh, he'll be back. His attachment to this little boy will keep him tied to Crystal Point."

"I'd like Oliver to know his uncle."

"Of course. You both have so little family it's important to keep in touch."

If it was a dig it was a soft one. And Cassie didn't mind. Ruthie Nevelson was like a grandmother to Tanner and she knew her motives were borne out of caring. Ruthie changed the subject and asked about her grandfather.

"He's not doing so well," she explained, remembering that Ruthie had known her granddad for many years. "I go and see him every week and sometimes he knows me and other times he doesn't."

Ruthie nodded. "It was good of Neville to take you in when your folks passed away. Especially when he was grieving the loss of his only son. I believe your grandmother had died only a year earlier."

"That's right. Gran had a seizure and died unexpectedly. Then my parents..." Her words trailed for a moment. "He was strong back then. And kind. He made a home for me and did his best. But I know the end is coming and as much as I'm prepared for it, I can't quite believe that once he's gone there'll only be Oliver and myself left in my family."

"Then you should get married and have a whole bunch of kids," Ruthie suggested. "I keep telling Tanner the same thing. Let this lonely old woman be a lesson to you." She gestured to their surroundings. "No point in having all this if you've no one to leave it to."

Marriage? More children? It was a lovely dream. "You're right. And I will." She smiled. "I promise."

"Watch making promises to Ruthie," a deep voice said from the doorway. "She'll hold you to them."

Ruthie guffawed and the sound made Cassie smile. Tanner stepped into the room and dropped his hat on the counter. Oliver squealed delightedly when he recognized him.

"Hey, little man," Tanner said and reached for him immediately. "Come here."

"See," Cassie complained lightheartedly. "I'm forgotten once he claps eyes on his favorite uncle."

Oliver was so happy to see Tanner it made her heart ache. And she was glad her son had someone else to love and protect him.

The only thing was, she wished she had someone like that, too.

"I'll make coffee and we'll go and sit in the front room."

"I really can't stay," Cassie said. "I have to—"

"Nonsense," Ruthie scolded gently. "I'd like to get to know Oliver a little better. And it's Saturday... What's more important than spending time with family on the weekend?"

She had a point. Even if thinking of Ruthie as family was a stretch. But she was family to Tanner, so Cassie wasn't about to argue the point. "Okay. I'll stay."

"Good," Ruthie said and pulled a tray down from a cupboard. "You two go on ahead and I'll bring it in."

Tanner was grinning, as if he knew exactly how it was to deny Ruthie Nevelson anything and not get your own way. He carried Oliver down the hallway and into the front living room. Cassie followed and stilled when she reached the doorway. The silky oak furniture and tapestries were magnificent and she let out a sigh.

"This is such a beautiful house."

Tanner was by the fireplace. "It became a home to me after my parents died."

Cassie crossed her arms. "We really did have similar childhoods. I mean, I know you were sent away to school, but you had a strong role model in Ruthie, like I did with my grandfather. Did you know our birthdays are only four days apart? I remember Doug telling me that a long time ago. We'll both be thirty-one next month."

He didn't say anything. He didn't move other than to gently rub the back of Oliver's head. Cassie looked at him and felt the heat in his stare.

It certainly hasn't been easy being attracted to you...

His words swirled around in her head. His confession should have sent her running. But she was inexplicably drawn to him. Like air to lungs. Like water to sand. Tanner McCord had awakened her sleeping libido with a resounding thud.

"How's your cheek?" she asked quietly.

"I'll live."

"I've never hit anyone before," she admitted. "You know, no siblings to wrestle with...no fights in the playground. That was my first slug."

"It was a good one."

She smiled and moved into the room. "Did you and Doug fight much?"

"No," he replied. "I guess the age difference made it hard to have the usual brother-on-brother wrestling matches. I did break his nose when I was eighteen, though."

Her eyes widened and she recalled Doug's slightly crooked nose. "On purpose?"

"Yeah. He hammered me afterward, but I still managed to get one good punch in."

Cassie grinned. "Well, I'm sure you had your reasons, considering the history."

He rocked Oliver gently in his arms and Cassie's heart wrenched seeing them together. He'd make such a good dad one day. She almost told him so, but stopped herself. There was enough tension between them without him mistakenly thinking she was lining him up as a candidate to be Oliver's father.

Which I'm not.

She shrugged and started looking at the rows of photographs above the fireplace and another row on the sideboard. There were pictures of Ruthie and her husband. Snapshots of horses and dogs and cattle. And there were some of Tanner, too. One from when he was at school and a few she recognized from the albums Doug had kept. A photo at the back caught her attention. It was obviously Tanner as a teenager, all rangy shoulders and long legs, wearing a plaid shirt and jeans and a cowboy hat. He stood beside a horse, a tall, pale coffee-colored animal that somehow tripped a wire in her brain. And a memory.

I know that horse...

I know that boy...

And then, like a speedy camera rolling out in reverse, realization hit.

The beach. The horse. The boy.

The kiss...

Cassie snapped her head around and stared at him. His

dark eyes narrowed just a fraction, enough for her to read the truth in them. He knew. He'd known all along.

"Oh, my God…that was you?" Her head reeled, her heart pounded. "That day on the beach…when we were young…you were the boy I…"

It made perfect, impossible sense. There had always been something familiar about Tanner. A kind of hazy awareness she couldn't decipher. Now she knew why. He *was* familiar. He was *that* boy. She looked at her son, so happy and content in Tanner's arms. Resentment flared and she quickly moved across the room and took her baby from his arms.

"I have to get out of here," she said and took a step toward the door.

He grasped her arm. "Cassie, wait—"

"Don't you get it?" she said, pulling free. "Every time I've been around you, I've always had this…feeling. This sense that I *know* you. It's twisted at my insides since that first time you came to visit Doug. I thought… I thought that I was just so attracted to you it made me imagine things. And I felt such guilt because I was with Doug and I shouldn't have been thinking that about someone else in that way…in *any* way. But it wasn't that at all. It was the memory of some silly schoolgirl infatuation when I was thirteen. It was some romantic fantasy I'd created in my head about being swept off my feet. And it stayed with me all my life. Even when I was with Doug, *especially* when I was with Doug, I was always comparing it to that feeling… that *fleeting* feeling I had when I was this lonely, love-struck thirteen-year-old crushing on the guy who kissed me for the very first time."

Within minutes she was out the room, out the door and in her car.

And driving away from the boy who'd captured her heart and the one man who had the power to break it.

Chapter Eight

Late on Sunday afternoon Lauren and Mary-Jayne arrived with pizza and sweet wine for their regular monthly get-together. Since Lauren's engagement and Oliver's birth they didn't catch up as often as they used to. However, they always made the most of their Sunday catch-up. It was over her first glass of wine and second slice of pizza that she told them about Tanner.

"That was him?" Lauren asked incredulously, eyes popping. "The boy on the beach?"

"Yeah…that was Tanner."

M.J. let out a long whistle. "What a tangled web we weave. Who would have thought that your first love would end up being *the jerk's* baby brother?"

"It wasn't love," Cassie corrected, ignoring the gibe about Doug. "We were kids and I only met him twice. And it was just a kiss."

"A kiss you've never forgotten," Lauren reminded her.

Cassie shrugged. "Every girl remembers her first kiss."

"Yeah," M.J. said and laughed. "But most of us would rather forget it. If I could erase the memory of Bobby Milton and his sweaty top lip I would do it gladly."

M.J. pretended to gag and they all giggled like teenagers. It felt so good to be with her friends. They shared a bond that had lasted decades. They'd rallied around her when Doug had been killed and then when Oliver was born. And she needed their support now, more than ever.

"So, are you going to kiss him again?" M.J. asked bluntly.

Cassie almost spat out her drink. "Of course not."

"Why not?" Lauren said. "He seems very nice and he's clearly interested in you."

"Because there's no point," she said quickly. "He's going back to South Dakota in a few weeks and the only thing I have time for is finding a new home for me and my son."

"A lot can happen in a few weeks," Lauren said and smiled. "Take it from me. It only took me that long to fall in love with Gabe."

"That was different," she said, holding on to her impatience. "Since you were looking for a relationship and I'm not. All I want is to find a home where I can live and raise my child. Do I like Tanner? Yes. Is he gorgeous and sexy and wonderful with Oliver? Yes. Do I think there's a future there? No. He's Doug's brother and that's simply too big a complication."

"Who are you trying to convince?" M.J. asked with a raised brow. "Us or yourself?"

Cassie ate some pizza and ignored her friend's gibe. They'd support her regardless. That was the way of best friends. "I know what I'm doing," she said.

But didn't believe it for a minute.

* * *

On Monday morning Tanner arrived at the house at nine o'clock with a painting contractor. The two men walked around the house discussing walls and ceilings and which rooms needed doing while Cassie remained in the kitchen with Oliver and felt like a spare part.

It's not my house... Remember that.

When the contractor left Tanner came into the kitchen and stood on the other side of the counter. "He'll be back on Wednesday morning. I thought we'd start in the bedrooms and work from the rear of the house."

"We?" she queried and sank her hands into the sinkful of soapy water. "There's not a whole lot of *we* in this, Tanner. It's your house, not mine. All I do is pay the rent and utilities. Which I'll continue to do until I find somewhere else to live. Paint whatever rooms you like, it makes no difference to me. I'll be out of here soon enough."

"You can stay until it sells."

"I'd prefer to leave as soon as I can."

"You mean you'd prefer to be stubborn and provocative."

She glared at him. "I'm not stubborn. And I'm definitely not provocative."

"Oh, yeah," he said and rested his hands on the counter. "You are."

"And you have an arrogant streak a mile wide," she yelled. "Contrary to what you might believe, you don't know what's best for me and Oliver. So back off."

He laughed loudly. "Why are you so mad at me? I'm only trying to help."

"Help someone else. I don't need or want anything from you."

"Where's all this resentment coming from, Cassie?" he

inquired, laughter still lingering in his eyes. "I thought we were friends."

Cassie pulled her hands from the sink, dried them quickly, then slammed them onto her hips. "You've got some nerve, you know that? After what happened the other day I'd think you would be—"

"So we made out when we were kids," he interrupted. "It's no big deal."

"No big deal?" she echoed. "Are you kidding? It's a huge deal. You knew. All along you knew and you didn't say anything."

He shrugged. "There was no point. And it was hardly a subject to broach when Doug was alive. We shared a kiss, Cassie. A long time ago. A lifetime ago. Forget about it."

She wished she could. "What about the other thing?"

"What other thing?"

Cassie inhaled, steadying her nerve. "You said you were attracted to me and—"

"So I'm attracted to you," he said quietly. "Stop over-thinking it."

"I can't." She crossed her arms over her chest. "And I can't believe you think it's okay and can dismiss it so easily."

"Did I say that?" he asked. "Did I once say it was okay? For the record—nothing is easy when it comes to you." He took a deep breath. "Yes, I'm attracted to you. Yes, I want to take you to bed and make love to you."

He heart stalled. "But—"

"But I know I can never do that because you love my brother."

Doug...

Had she spared him a thought since she'd seen Tanner on Saturday? Her feelings for Doug were so conflicted. And the more she knew Tanner the less she felt she knew Doug.

"I don't think... I mean, we'd be crazy to start something," she whispered. "And now that I have Oliver I can't afford to act crazy."

"I agree," he said flatly. "Forget it, like I said. I'll be gone in a few weeks and then you can get on with the rest of your life."

Sure. No problem.

And she knew he believed that about as much as she did.

Midweek Tanner took a call from the foreman at his ranch and discussed the new horses that were coming in over the next two months. His leg still hurt and he intended getting back to physical therapy when he returned home, but working with Ruthie's colt had confirmed that he was ready to get back in the saddle.

And it made him miss home. His ranch in Cedar Creek was as much a part of him as Crystal Point had been when he was young, and being in the small town had brought back a whole lot of memories. Some good. Some not. Hanging out with Ruthie was a bonus. So was spending time with his nephew. Oliver had quickly worked his way into his heart and Tanner knew he was going to miss the little guy when he returned to South Dakota.

And then there was Cassie...

She'd gotten into his heart, too, and he was trying his damnedest to get her out.

Her home was being sold and she had put on a brave face...but he wasn't fooled. And he felt a ton of guilt because of it. While the contractor worked on the house she kept insisting she was fine. While painters and yard maintenance workers came and went she was on hand making iced tea and obligingly moving belongings from one room to the next. And he still wasn't fooled. She could act as tough and indifferent as she wanted; Tanner knew that underneath she was barely hanging on.

"You know," she said on Friday afternoon as they inspected the paintwork in the third bedroom. "You're really lousy at choosing colors. What is that feature wall color... mission brown?"

"Donkey," he replied and shrugged. "And I did ask you to come with me and choose the palette."

Her mouth drew together tightly and she raised one shoulder. "Not my business."

"Well, if the house doesn't go under the hammer because I'm a little color-blind and you weren't charitable enough to help out, then it's on your head."

She sniffed. "Color-blind? You mean you have imperfections? I don't believe it."

"I'm as imperfect as the next guy."

"Nice to know." She walked around the room. "I think this needs to be done again," she said as she inspected the longest wall. "To something lighter. It's like a big brown tomb in here."

Tanner grabbed a swatch palette from a bucket near the door and pulled his wallet from his back pocket. He took out a credit card and held it toward her along with the swatches. "It's in your hands, then."

She looked at the card and frowned. "You're giving me your credit card?"

"Giving?" he echoed. "No. Loaning...sure."

She took both and looked at him oddly. "Doug never..."

"Does everything have to be about Doug?" he growled irritably.

"No, of course not," she said quickly. "It's only that he would never have trusted me to..." She stopped and looked at him. "It's nothing. Forget I said anything."

"Yeah, forget I said anything, too… I didn't mean to snap at you. Now go and spend some money."

She smiled. "I'll try not to do anything too irresponsible with it."

"I'll bet you haven't had an irresponsible moment in your life."

She laughed lightly. "Probably. However, I may be responsible, but according to some I am stubborn."

"And provocative," he reminded her.

She grinned, pushing the card into the pocket of her jeans as she clasped the swatches under one arm. "I'm sorry I haven't been much help this week. I know I'd promised I would be. It's just…"

"Too hard?" he prompted. "Too real? I get it, Cassie. I understand how difficult this must be for you."

She sucked in a breath. "Would you stop that," she snapped.

"Stop what?"

"Being so bloody understanding," she replied hotly. "About the house, about Doug…about *everything*. It drives me crazy."

"I drive you crazy?"

"It," she corrected. "*It* drives me crazy. You…well, you do…other stuff."

Tanner laughed. It was the most lighthearted conversation they'd had all week. And he'd missed it. *A little harmless flirting is okay.* "What kind of stuff?"

"Like I'd admit to anything." She tapped her back pocket. "Can you watch Oliver for an hour or so? I've got shopping to do."

"Absolutely."

"I'll grab dinner while I'm out," she said and then stilled. "I mean, if you'd like to stay."

"I would."

She nodded and quickly left the room. While she was gone he fed and bathed Oliver and had him well-settled in his crib by the time her car pulled up in the driveway. She bought paint and Chinese food. He put the paint in the spare room and they ate dinner from the cartons in the living room.

"You're something of an expert with those chopsticks," she remarked as she dipped into a carton for a chicken dumpling with a fork.

"I spent some time traveling through Vietnam and Cambodia before I went to Europe when I was young. So I picked up a few tips."

"I envy you," she said and sat back on the sofa, cross-legged. "I've never traveled. I've never been anywhere, really."

"Nothing wrong with being happy where you are."

"Happy or complacent?" She sighed. "I'm not sure I'd know the difference."

"You'd know," he assured her. "And as much as I enjoyed traveling, I was keen to put down roots when I reached South Dakota."

"Tell me about your ranch?"

"It's small by local standards," he said and drank some soda. "But the grazing is good for horses. The homestead is way too big for one, though."

"But one day you'll get married and have a family…so big will come in handy."

"I guess. One day."

"Have you ever been close?" she asked.

"To getting married? No."

She smiled a little. "Why not? You'd be something of a catch, I would think."

Tanner laughed. "I think… I think it's because I don't want to settle…if that makes sense. I remember my parents had a very strong relationship, grounded in friendship but also passionate. So I guess that's what I'm hoping for, too."

She sighed heavily. "Soul mates, you mean. Yeah, it's a nice dream."

"You don't believe in soul mates?"

"I do… I just don't know how many actually end up together. Although my friends Lauren and Gabe managed to find one another. So perhaps there's hope for us all."

"And you and Doug?"

She met his gaze. "I think you know the answer to that."

"He did love you," Tanner said quietly, absorbing her features in the lamplight. "In his own way. As much as he could love anyone."

She shrugged. "It doesn't really matter much anymore. I have Oliver and I will always be thankful to Doug for that."

Tanner heard the rawness in her voice and winced. "He was never the settle-down type, that's all. After our parents died all he wanted to do was leave Crystal Point for good."

"And that's when he sold your family farm, dumped you in boarding school and then a few years later squandered your inheritance?" Her brows came up. "What did he actually do with the money?"

"Some poor stock market decisions saw off most of it. A bit of gambling. I believe he bought a Porsche and crashed it." Tanner grinned and raised the chopsticks. "You know, the usual stuff. I was surprised when he bought this house…seemed way too sensible."

"And me?" she asked softly. "Were you surprised about me?"

Tanner dropped the chopsticks into the carton and placed it on the coffee table. Then he sat back, linked his fingers together and rested his hands on his stomach. "That he would want you? Not at all. As far as I know you're the first woman he actually attempted to settle down with. But he was a strange contradiction. In the military he was one kind of man, and out of it he was kind of lost."

"You're very forgiving."

Tanner shook his head. "I'm not forgiving at all. But if I hang on to my resentment, then he wins. Bitterness is a wasted emotion. I'd rather look for—"

"Love?" she asked, quietly cutting off his words.

Tanner stilled. The way she said it. The way the word hung in the air between them made his gut churn. He didn't want to talk to her about love. Not when his heart was in the firing line. "Aren't we all?" he queried vaguely.

"I guess. Some more than others."

He got to his feet. "I should go. I'll see you tomorrow."

And he left before he said or did something stupid.

The following week blurred into one day after another. There were more contractors. More painting. More trucks coming and going as the backyard got a serious overhaul with some new garden beds and paving. Cassie put on her brave face and helped out where she could. But inside she was churning. Tanner was mostly on hand to give orders to the contractors and she gave him the spare key so he could come and go as needed. But he never stayed longer than necessary. He spent time with Oliver. He was polite and obliging to her and that was all. They didn't talk about Doug or anything other than the house. She noticed he was unusually quiet and seemed to have a lot on his mind. She didn't ask. Didn't want to know. He was leaving in two weeks and she'd become so accustomed to having him around she knew she'd feel his departure when he went home.

Home...

Something she didn't have anymore. She'd put in a couple of rental applications during that week. Since there was nothing she could reasonably afford in Crystal Point she looked at renting in Bellandale. It wasn't optimal. In fact, it wasn't what she wanted at all. But it would be closer to the hospital when she returned to work and there were a couple of reputable day care centers close by.

It's not worth crying over...

On Saturday afternoon the last of the contractors left for the day and once Oliver was down for his nap she fed Mouse and then drew herself a long bath. By four she was in the kitchen, lazing around in her bathrobe and snacking on cheese and crackers. She was in the middle of filling the kettle when the doorbell rang. Thinking it might be Mary-Jayne stopping in for an impromptu visit, she steadied the towel she'd wrapped around her hair to keep her tresses dry, padded down the hallway on bare feet and opened the door.

And then rocked back on her heels.

It was Tanner. And he looked so gorgeous it stole her breath.

Usually he dressed in faded jeans and T-shirts. But the man who stood at her door looked as if he'd stepped out of the pages of a cowboy magazine. His jeans were dark and tailored and the white twill shirt fit across his shoulders, tapering down over his chest and washboard belly. He wore a thin leather bolo tie and a thick leather belt with a shimmering silver buckle and cowboy boots. He held a felt hat in one hand and car keys in the other.

Cassie swallowed hard. "Oh...hi."

He looked her over in a kind of slow, leisurely way that made her toes curl. The bathrobe was thin, and knowing there was only a light layer of fabric covering her nakedness quickly increased her awareness of him.

"Hello. Can I come in?"

She pulled the front of her robe secure and opened the

screen. "Of course." Once he was in the hall she asked the obvious question. "What are you doing here?"

Tanner dropped his keys and hat onto the hall stand. "I thought we could go out."

What did that mean? She tilted her head, and as the towel fell in her hands her hair cascaded around her shoulders. The movement seemed to stop him in his tracks. He watched her intently and heat quickly fanned through her blood. *One look,* she thought. *That's all it takes.* Damn Tanner McCord and his beautiful hide.

She quickly pulled herself together. "Out?"

"To the Rosemount Rodeo," he explained. "Ruthie's competing in a senior's team penning event and I thought it would be nice to cheer her on."

Which didn't explain why he was on her doorstep. "So, this would be a date?"

Color slashed his cheeks. He was embarrassed. Was she so *undatable*? "Well…no…only in the way that we'd be together."

"Like a date?" she said and smiled, and then let him off the hook. "I can't get a sitter for Oliver at this time of—"

"The baby comes, too, of course," he said. "It's something of a family event anyhow. He'll be quite safe."

Cassie shook her head. "I don't know… I've only just put him down for a nap and I'm not dressed and I probably—"

"I'll wait," he said easily.

She was about to refuse and then changed her mind. What was the harm? And it beat spending another lonely Saturday night alone. "Okay. Give me half an hour."

It took nearly forty minutes, but by then she was changed into a long denim skirt and pale blue sweater and had put on makeup, styled her hair and got Oliver ready.

"Impressive," Tanner remarked when she came into the living room. "Just over half an hour and you're done."

"Thirty-eight minutes, to be exact. So, are we taking my car or yours?"

"Mine," he replied. "I had a baby seat fitted this morning."

Cassie didn't hide her surprise. "You did? Why?"

He shrugged loosely. "For Oliver. I'll leave it with you when I go home."

Cassie tried to ignore the way her insides contracted at the idea of him returning to South Dakota. Of course she knew it was inevitable. He would leave and she and Oliver would be alone again.

Once they were outside, he lifted Oliver from her arms and gently strapped him into the baby seat she recognized as an expensive brand and one she hadn't been able to afford when she'd purchased the basic model that was buckled in the back of her old Honda.

"Incidentally," he said once the back was shut and he'd opened the passenger door, "you look lovely."

Cassie blushed. "You don't look so bad yourself, cowboy."

It was the grandest of understatements. In all her life Cassie had never found any man as attractive as she found Tanner. He was handsome, for sure, but there was something about him that appealed to her on a sensory level. While Doug had been charming and loud and always looking for attention, his brother was quieter and clearly more at home in his own skin. Gone was her idea that Tanner was some kind of disinterested loner. He was, in fact, the complete opposite. He liked company. He was funny and kind and just a little bullheaded and the more time she spent with him the more she liked him.

More than that.

Cassie knew she was in danger of falling for him…and it scared her to pieces.

By the time they reached the Rosemount Rodeo the sun was going down. There was a show ground attached to the horse arena and Cassie spotted a Ferris wheel and a few other recognizable carnival rides. A male voice was talking on the loudspeaker and there was music coming from a small stadium behind a sideshow alley. Tanner found a parking space close to the entrance gates, and once they got Oliver settled in his stroller he called Ruthie on the phone and they made their way toward the rows of stables and corrals. They stopped by the competitors' gate and waited.

"Ruthie should be along soon. She's only in one event," he explained and positioned himself in front of her and the stroller so they were out of the way of horses and riders passing by.

Cassie didn't mind. Having grown up in Crystal Point, the smell of horses and cattle was a familiar one and she liked the carnival atmosphere created by the riders, spectators and animals.

"It's fine," she said and smiled. "Thanks for getting me out of the house. I've become something of a hermit since Oliver was born."

"Managing a newborn alone couldn't have been easy."

She shrugged and glanced at Oliver gurgling happily in his stroller. "I had Lauren and M.J. on standby if I needed help. And he's such a good baby I really can't complain."

"You're an excellent mom," he said softly and touched her shoulder. "He's a lucky kid."

"Thanks," she said and felt the heat of his touch right through to her bones. "But I'm simply flying by the seat of my pants. He makes it easy. And you've made it easier, too," she said, smiling as she reached up and laid her hand on his chest. His heart pounded beneath her palm. The beat was strong and steady. Like everything about him. "So, thank you."

"Tanner!"

At the sound of someone calling his name she dropped her hand to her side like a stone. They both turned to find a middle-aged couple standing about twenty feet away, waving their arms in a way that indicated they knew him. She looked at Tanner and saw his expression harden instantly.

"Be back in a minute," he said and began to move off.

Cassie grasped his arm. "Is everything okay?"

"Fine," he assured her and gently removed her hand. "Stay here. I'll be back soon."

She stayed put and watched him stride across the gravel. The couple, a man and woman in their late fifties, greeted him with what looked like genuine joy. She watched with interest as he shook the man's hand and lightly kissed the woman's cheek. So, he did know them. And quite well by the look of things. She pushed back the tiny surge of exclusion and fiddled with the strap on her tote while keeping a discreet eye on Tanner and his friends.

"There you are!"

Ruthie Nevelson's voice quickly distracted her. The older woman was striding toward her, dressed in moleskins, a bright orange shirt and fancy vest with diamantés sewn across the lapel.

"Hi, Ruthie."

She reached them and grinned widely. "I've been looking forward to seeing this young fella again." As she peered into the stroller, Oliver gurgled. "I'm pleased Tanner talked you into coming."

"Me, too," she said and smiled.

"Where is he?"

Cassie pointed to where he stood, now deep in conversation with his friends. "There."

Ruthie frowned and her hands moved to her bony hips. "Oh...I know them. That's Malcolm and Sue Stewart."

"Who?"

"Leah's parents. Awful business, what happened to that girl. Broke poor Tanner's heart. Worse thing he did was introduce her to that no good—" Ruthie stopped and looked as though she'd said something she shouldn't have. "I better get—"

"Who's Leah?" Cassie asked quickly, figuring she must have been more than a friend and getting more curious by the second.

Ruthie waved a hand dismissively. "Oh, just an old friend of Tanner's. Well, best I get back to my horse. I'll see you later at the dance."

"Dance?"

"Sure," she said and winked. "I'm going to watch this young man," she said and pointed to Oliver. "While you dance with that young man," she added and gestured toward Tanner. "See you later."

Once she'd disappeared from view Cassie turned her attention back to Tanner and saw he was now on his way back to her. When he reached her he was smiling, but Cassie saw the tension in his jaw.

"Sorry about that."

"Who are they?"

He shrugged. "Just some people I used to know."

"People?" Her brows came up.

"Parents of an old friend," he said vaguely. "We should go and get seated before—"

"Leah's parents?"

He stilled instantly. "How do you know that? Did Doug say something to you about—"

"What's Doug got to do with it?" she asked as her skin prickled with an unexpected sense of apprehension. "Ruthie was just here and said something about it. Tanner, who's Leah?" she asked again.

"Just an old friend, like I said."

"An old girlfriend?" she corrected, oblivious to the people walking by. "Right?"

"Yes."

"*Your* old girlfriend? And something bad happened to her?"

"I'd rather not—"

"Tell me," she insisted. "What happened? What's the big secret? Why did Ruthie look like she'd said something she shouldn't?"

"I have no idea," he said flatly. "And it's not important so let's—"

"Leah was your girlfriend?" she asked, pushing relentlessly for more information. "And then?"

His eyes darkened so they were almost black and his jaw looked so tight it could have been carved from granite. "She got pregnant and lost the baby. Afterward she had a kind of breakdown and has been in and out of hospitals ever since."

Cassie gripped his forearm. "Oh, God, Tanner...I'm so sorry. I didn't know you'd lost a child. Now I understand why it's so important to you that Oliver—"

His expression was unreadable as he shook his head. "*I* didn't lose a child. She did. The baby wasn't mine."

Cassie's blood stilled in her veins. "Not yours? Then who...?"

As her words trailed the thought of the most unimaginable betrayal flashed through her mind. *No.* It couldn't be. She looked at him and shook her head, not wanting to believe it.

But saw the terrible truth in his eyes.

Chapter Nine

"It was Doug?"

Tanner flinched. "Yes."

She looked at him, her eyes huge in her face and every old hurt he'd ever felt he saw in her expression. "That's the history between you… It's not about the inheritance. It was about a girl?"

He nodded and reached down to ease Oliver from the stroller. "She fell in love with him. We were young and just out of school and I guess he was older and experienced and more exciting to her."

"Did Doug love her, too?"

"He never said," Tanner replied, hating how the lie tasted in his mouth. Doug had said he'd loved Leah. Just as he'd said he'd loved Cassie. But he wasn't about to tell her any more. Or how Doug had told Leah to terminate her pregnancy and then promptly broke off their affair when she said she wanted to keep the baby. Cassie would work out the pattern of Doug's behavior in a heartbeat.

He held Oliver close to his chest and experienced an almost painful surge of love for the little boy. He remembered how Leah's parents had remarked what a lovely family he had and Tanner hadn't corrected them.

If only it were true...

If Cassie and Oliver were his he would never let them go. But they weren't. She'd loved Doug. As Leah had.

Admit it...you'd be her consolation prize.

"He never told me any of this," she said. "Not a word. I didn't know him at all."

Tanner wasn't about to agree with her. "Come on, let's get seated. We don't want to miss Ruthie's ride."

"Tanner, I—"

"Later," he said and grabbed her hand. "This isn't the place to have this discussion. We'll talk about it later."

She nodded and they walked into the stands, finding a spot that was close to the exit in case they needed to leave in a hurry. Ruthie's event was on a few minutes later and Tanner watched with pride as his friend came out and cut the tagged beasts out of the herd, and then worked with her team to corral them well within the allocated time.

Afterward, they headed for the sideshow alley, where Tanner won a stuffed pelican for Oliver on the horseshoe toss and a pair of oversize hot-pink sunglasses for Cassie on the rifle range. They spent a leisurely hour together and it only served to amplify every buried feeling he had for her. He fought the urge to hold her hand and instead carried Oliver while she perused the craft stalls. He knew she was tense. He could see it in her walk and the tight way she held her shoulders back. And he knew she was thinking about Doug. And about Leah.

But it wasn't the time or place to have that conversation.

When she was done with the sideshow ally they made their way toward the food tent, and once they found seats he bought them burgers and fries while she gave Oliver his bottle. Ruthie turned up and when they finished eating they all moved to where the band was playing. By now Oliver was asleep and tucked in his stroller, and Ruthie waved them onto the dance floor.

"Are you sure?" Cassie asked him. "Your leg isn't—"

"It's fine," he lied, thinking his leg ached like the devil because he'd done way too much walking for one evening. But the idea of holding Cassie in his arms just once was too tempting to refuse. She didn't protest and when they reached the dance floor the song changed to a slower ballad.

"I did warn you, remember," she reminded him, "that I couldn't dance."

Tanner smiled and drew her in his arms. "And remember what I said? Just sway."

He wrapped his arms around her and could feel every lovely curve as he drew her closer. Tanner rested one hand on her hip and linked the other with hers. They danced slowly, not speaking, just moving together as if they'd danced a hundred times before. It struck him profoundly how effortless it was to be with her. How natural it was to hold her. And how easy it would be to kiss her. When the song ended she pulled back and looked up at him.

"Thank you," she said. "It's been a long time since I've done that. But I think I'd like to go now. We really need to talk and I'd like to do it at home."

Tanner nodded and they left the dance floor. It took fifteen minutes to say their goodbyes to Ruthie, collect Oliver and head back to the car. And another thirty minutes to reach Crystal Point. He pulled into the driveway and once they were out of the car she took the baby inside and put him to bed. By the time he'd fed Mouse and let the dog outside, she was in the lounge room, pacing the floor.

"Is Oliver settled?" he asked from the doorway.

"Yes." She remained standing, arms crossed, chin raised. "Did you find out about what Doug had done with Leah before or after he stole your inheritance?"

Straight to the point. A trait of hers he'd come to recognize. "After. Before. It was all around the same time."

Her gaze narrowed. "So, he stole your money and your girlfriend and got her pregnant?"

"Yes."

She dropped down onto the love seat in the corner. "I think I need to throw up."

Tanner moved into the room and stood behind the sofa. "It was a long time ago."

"Which doesn't change how utterly despicable it was."

"No," he said. "But time does alter perspective on things."

She shook her head and stared at him. "So you simply forgive and forget and move on?"

"Or get bogged down with anger and resentment," he replied. "And that's no way to live."

She twisted her hands in her lap. "I feel like… I feel like I suddenly know nothing of the man I knew, the man who fathered my son. The man you describe…he's a stranger. He's a cold, unfeeling stranger who did whatever he wanted and didn't care who got hurt in the process."

"Then don't remember him that way," Tanner said and came around the sofa. "Remember him as the man who made you laugh. The man you loved."

"How can I?" she implored. "I'd be living a lie. How could I love a man who did such things? That would make me…pathetic."

"Or human."

She jumped to her feet. "Stop that. Stop making excuses... for Doug...for me. Stop being so forgiving and get mad at him!"

The passion in her voice shifted the mood in the room on some kind of invisible axis. Tanner stared at her, wholly aware of her in a deep, soul-wrenching way. She was angry and confused and he watched as her rage gathered momentum. He knew that about her. He knew she was passionate and spirited and not the quiet wallflower his brother had often described. Around him she was fiery and full of life. She was combative and argumentative and stirred his blood and libido. And he wanted her. In his arms. In his bed. In his life.

Suddenly she was in front of him, hands on hips, her cheeks ablaze, chest heaving as she drew in large gulps of air. Heat swirled between them and without thinking he grasped her shoulders and pulled her close. Her arms dropped and then she was against him, breast to chest. And he claimed her lips. As he'd done when they were thirteen. As he'd imagined a thousand times since.

And she kissed him back. She opened her mouth and let him inside. She wound her tongue around his and groaned low in her throat when his hands moved down her arms and settled around her back, drawing her closer. There was heat and passion and urgency in the kiss. And it went on and on. He didn't stop. She didn't pull away. Her hands were on his shoulders and she sighed against his mouth in complete and utter surrender.

And in that moment Tanner knew he was done for.

He loved her.

And there was no going back. Nowhere to run. No part of his mind or body that could conceal what he'd tried so hard to deny for so long.

"Cassandra..." He whispered her full name against her

lips. "Let me stay tonight. I want to make love to you so much."

And that's when she froze.

She wrenched free and stepped back. "Why?" she asked, breathless and suspicious.

Tanner stared at her. "Why?" He repeated her question. "Why do you think?"

She took another step backward. "That's what I'm asking. Why?" She took a deep breath. "Payback maybe?"

"Payback? What does that mean?"

"You get into my bed," she shot back, eyes blazing, "like Doug got into Leah's all those years ago."

Disbelief surged through him. "That's ridiculous. You don't actually believe I would do that to you?"

"I don't know what to believe anymore," she said, shaking her head. "I didn't think Doug was the kind of man to betray his only brother in such a terrible way…but I was wrong. And I'd known him for three years. And since I've really only known you for two weeks how can I be sure of your motives?" She moved to the mantel and waved a hand past Doug's photo. "All I know is that I'm not going to make a mistake that will end up with me having all these… *feelings*…and then end up looking like a first-rate fool."

Tanner's heart thumped in his chest. "You think making love with me would be a mistake?"

"I think making love with you would be out of this world," she said quietly. "And then I'd wake up in the morning and remember you are leaving soon. And then I'd also remember that Doug treated you badly and it would make perfect sense that you'd want a little revenge."

Tanner rocked back on his boots. "I don't want revenge. I never did."

"Then what do you want?" she shot back. "A ready-made family? Because that's what you get with me, Tanner. You get me and Oliver. Your brother's *leftover* family. The family he never got to claim because he was killed. How could you possibly want that? Not after what he did to you. Even I'm not *that* naive."

Tanner heard the pain in her words. Felt them through to his bones. The truth about Doug teetered on his lips. But he could never tell her that his brother had no intention of claiming her and Oliver. Even if she suspected it, he couldn't tell her. Hurting Cassie was the last thing he would intentionally do. It didn't matter how he felt…Doug would *always* be between them.

It was insurmountable. Impossible. And foolhardy to think otherwise.

"I'll see myself out," he said flatly. "Good night."

He didn't wait for a response and it took less than a minute to get to his car and drive off.

"So, what happened then?"

Cassie wasn't the kiss-and-tell type. But she'd needed someone to talk to and M.J. was her friend, even though the other woman usually dished out the kind of advice she often didn't want to hear. The alternative was to speak to Lauren. But she was happily wrapped up in her fairy-tale engagement with Gabe Vitali, so Cassie figured M.J. was the better option.

"After we kissed?"

Just thinking of the kiss they'd shared made her head spin. It would have been so easy to let him stay.

"Yeah," M.J. said and sighed. "After the kiss, what then?"

"We just came to our senses."

"You did or he did?"

"Both," she replied and poured a second round of coffee for them both. "The truth is I don't know how to feel about him."

"Because of Doug?"

"Because of *him*," she replied. "Because he's only here temporarily. Because he's handsome and nice and so incredible with Oliver that I could easily fall… You know what I mean."

"Fall in love?"

"Yeah," she admitted, terrified to even imagine the idea. "I was so close to saying yes when Tanner said he wanted to stay the night with me. But I was so scared about what it would mean. For him. For me. Even for Oliver. Sex would just complicate things even more than they already are."

"Sex usually does," M.J. said with a wry smile. "But if you like him…"

"I do like him. That's the trouble."

"I think the trouble is that you're scared of loving anyone again," M.J. said astutely. "Doug wasn't exactly Mr. Commitment or Mr. Reliable and you're afraid that Tanner won't be, either."

"But he is," she said and sipped her coffee. "That's the thing…I know he's different from Doug but I'm still unsure. I'm still scared."

"Well, no one ever said love was rational. Maybe you simply need to talk to him again. Have you seen him since?"

Cassie shook her head. She hadn't seen Tanner for two days. "He's probably avoiding me. The house painting and the gardens have been finished so there's no need for him to be here."

"I saw the for-sale sign out front. I'm sorry."

She sighed. "Well, I knew it was coming. The real estate people came through last week and took pictures and the sign went up early this morning. I almost wish it sells quickly so I'm forced to find somewhere straightaway. I've had no luck leasing a new house. The two I applied for that I can afford won't take a dog. So I'm back trawling the listings again."

"Something will turn up," M.J. assured her. "And I can always take Mouse if it comes to that."

"I know," Cassie said and sighed. "But I need to stand on my own two feet. And that means finding a place for myself, my son and my dog—all of whom are my responsibility. As for Tanner...he'll be gone soon. I doubt he'll stay until the house sells. He's got his ranch to get back to. And his life. And I'm just a little blip on his radar."

"Are you sure about that?"

"I'm not sure about anything," she admitted. "But I do know I'm not courageous enough to lay myself on the line. Been there, done that."

M.J. came around the counter and gave her a much-needed hug. "I still think you should talk to him. Sticking your head in the sand didn't do you any favors when it came to Doug. And it won't do you any favors with Tanner, either."

"I know. But I'm not that brave."

"Sure you are," her friend said gently. "You're as brave as they come. Make the call and talk to him. You never know what might happen."

That's the problem...

How could she explain how scared she was? Or how confused she was about Tanner? Cassie took a long breath and nodded. "Okay. I will."

But she didn't. Because late that afternoon her grandfather had a massive stroke and was rushed to intensive care. Cassie dropped Oliver at Lauren's and rushed to the hospital, where she found her grandfather fighting for his life in a hospital room, his frail body connected to tubes and monitors. The doctor saw her immediately and gave her the grim news. It didn't look good and her grandfather was critical. He probably wouldn't wake up. There wasn't anything they could do and she needed to prepare herself. She needed to say goodbye.

Then they let her see him. She touched his forehead and told him she loved him. She thanked him for being a loving, caring grandparent and hoped in some way he heard and understood her words.

After a while, with her emotions at breaking point, she got up and headed out to the waiting room. She was still sitting there at eight o'clock. Still there as other worried relatives, other families, came and went. Still there as nurses changed shifts. And still there when a tall, jeans-clad figure came into the room and sat down beside her. She didn't move. Didn't speak. But a welcome relief washed over her the moment Tanner reached out and grasped her hand, enfolding it within his.

"How did you—"

"I spoke to Lauren," he explained softly. "She told me you were here."

Cassie nodded and heat prickled behind her eyes. "I'm so sick and tired of death," she said, her throat thick. "I mean, I knew this day was coming. In my mind I've been prepared for it in a hundred ways. But right now, right here, all I can think is how I'm so tired of losing the people I love. I'm tired of loss and grief. Every time I lose someone I feel my world getting smaller...because I'm just that little bit more alone."

He squeezed her hand and she experienced a connection deep down. "You're not alone."

For now...

But she didn't say it. All she could do was remember their kiss. Remember how she'd felt in his arms.

Complete...

That's how he made her feel. In a way no man ever had before. Not even Doug. Cassie dropped her head to his shoulder and closed her eyes. He was strong, a rock, a haven for her fragile heart when she needed comfort and understanding. And he knew it. Their connection was deep, borne out of sharing a similar road in life. They could, she suspected, become the firmest of friends. And lovers. And more.

And it terrified her.

Cassie believed she'd loved Doug. He'd turned up in her life at a time she'd been vulnerable and alone, and for a while he'd made her feel as if she was part of something. A couple. A family. But deep in her heart she'd never felt truly cherished. Yet she hadn't questioned his commitment, even as he drifted back and forth into her life during the brief years they were together. She accepted it. Blindly. Foolishly. Because she'd never truly believed she deserved more from him...or from anyone.

Knowing what Doug was really like had changed that. She *did* deserve more. Only, she was too scared to trust what her heart and body yearned for.

When the doctor returned half an hour later and told them her grandfather had passed away, Cassie gripped Tanner's hand as hard as she could. He sat with her for a while and then later he drove her car back to Crystal Point and left his rental in the hospital car park. They stopped by Lauren's and Cassie remained in the car while Tanner collected her son. Lauren didn't come out and Cassie was grateful. She didn't need sympathy. She didn't want hugs and kind words. She wanted the comfort of silence. And the strength of broad shoulders that she knew instinctively would be there if she needed them.

Tanner didn't say a word on the drive home, nor when

he took a sleeping Oliver from the backseat and followed her wordlessly up the path and then inside. He put Oliver to bed and found her on the sofa in the living room, hands tucked in her lap.

"The baby's asleep," he said. "You should get some rest, too... You'll have a hard day tomorrow."

She knew that. There were plans to be made. A funeral to arrange. Her grandfather's things to collect from the nursing home. Cassie nodded and stood as a lethargic numbness crept over her skin and seeped into her blood.

"Thank you for being with me tonight."

He didn't move from his spot by the door. "Go and sleep. I'll tend to the baby when he wakes during the night."

"I can't ask you to—"

"You're not," he said, cutting her off. "Go to bed, Cassie. I'll see you in the morning."

She stood and walked toward him, all her emotional strength zapped and with no energy to disagree. "Okay. Thanks."

He reached out and held the back of her neck for a moment, rubbing her skin with his thumb. Then he softly kissed her forehead. "Good night."

Cassie walked down the hallway to her bedroom, closed the door and dropped onto the bed. She tried to cry. She tried to weep away the pain in her heart. But no tears came.

Neville Duncan's funeral was a somber affair. Around one hundred and fifty people turned up for the service and most stayed for the wake held underneath a canopy in the gardens of the chapel at the cemetery. Cassie was stoic the entire afternoon and Tanner kept a close and watchful eye over her as she politely thanked her grandfather's friends for coming.

Once the wake was over about twenty of her friends

and some colleagues from work came back to the house, where Lauren's mother had arranged for a catered meal for another, more intimate gathering. Tanner kept Oliver in his arms for most of the day and was feeding the baby in the kitchen when Ruthie spoke from the doorway.

"He's very attached to you."

Tanner looked up and smiled. "It's mutual."

Ruthie came into the room and rested her hands on the back of a chair. "You plannin' on sticking around longer than you'd thought?"

"Not at this stage. The house is on the market, so we'll see what happens."

Her gaze flicked to Oliver. "It's gonna be hard for you to leave. I mean, now you've got something to stay for."

He rocked Oliver gently. "I'll come back to see him when I can."

Ruthie cocked her head to one side. "That's not exactly what I meant. You still aiming to get your heart broken again?"

"Not a chance."

"Good," she said and smiled. "Now, get back to South Dakota, find yourself a wife and make a couple of these," Ruthie said and pointed to the baby. "Because this daddy stuff really suits you."

Tanner laughed softly. Ruthie had a way of cheering him up. And she was right. He loved hanging out with Oliver and being around him only confirmed what he'd begun to suspect—he was ready for his own family. After Ruthie left he put the baby in his crib and walked back into the front living room. There were only a few people remaining—Lauren and her fiancé, Gabe, M.J. and two older couples he remembered were Lauren's and M.J.'s parents. Cassie was by the window, sitting alone, her gaze focused on the teacup in her hand. He walked across the room and perched on the stool next to her.

"You okay?"

She looked up. "Sure."

"Oliver's in his crib, sleeping soundly."

She nodded. "Thank you for looking after him. It's been a busy day for him."

"He's handled it. He's tough…like his mom."

Her brows came up. "I'm not so tough. This is just my disguise."

Tanner glanced around the room. "Well, I don't think anyone has figured that out. And your secret is safe with me."

She leaned closer. "I wish…" Her whisper faded for a second. "I wish everyone would leave."

Tanner moved forward. "I'm not sure being alone is the—"

"I won't be alone," she said, interrupting him. "I have Oliver." She stopped and met his gaze. "And you."

Tanner's stomach clenched. All day she'd held it together, as he'd known she would. She'd spoken at the service, giving a short eulogy for her grandfather, and he'd marveled at her strength and resilience in the face of her grief. But he knew she was lost inside. He knew her heart was broken. And he wished he could fix her. He wished he could ease the pain in her heart and offer comfort. When all he could do, he knew, was simply be a friend. He couldn't hold her. He couldn't take her in his arms and stroke her skin and kiss her lips and help her forget her troubles.

It was another half an hour and nearly seven o'clock before the last guests left. By then he could see she was almost at the breaking point. Her back was ramrod straight, her arms clasped tightly around her waist and her eyes shadowed with a heavy, inconsolable pain.

Once the front door was closed and she'd waved off her friends she joined him in the kitchen, where he was stacking the dishwasher to keep his hands busy and his mind off taking her in his arms.

"Well," Cassie said with a weary sigh as she came around the counter. "I'm glad that's over."

"It's been a hard day. But I know your grandfather would have been very proud of you."

"I hope so."

He shut the dishwasher and straightened. "Do you need anything? Lauren's mother stored the leftovers in the fridge if you're hungry."

"I don't think my stomach would tolerate food at the moment."

"You should eat something."

"I can't…"

Her body shook slightly and as she gripped the back of a chair for support, Tanner raced around the counter and reached her in a few long strides.

"Cassie?"

She looked up and the tears in her eyes tore through him. "I feel so…"

"I know," he said and gathered her close. "I know, sweetheart."

She sighed heavily and pressed her face into his chest. And then she cried. Heavy, racking sobs that made him ache inside. Tanner cradled her head and held her, feeling her despair through to his bones. It was several minutes before she moved, and when he felt her resistance Tanner released her and she stepped back unsteadily.

"I'm sorry," she said with a hiccup as she wiped her cheeks. "I promised myself I wouldn't do that today."

"You're allowed to grieve, Cassie."

She shook her head. "That's just it…I'm tired of grieving. I grieved my parents and then Doug and now…this. I can't do it. I can't bear the hollow feeling and the sadness. It's too hard and it's not what I want."

"Then what do you want?"

She raised her chin. "I want to stop living my life like I'm all out of backbone."

"That's not what—"

"It is," she insisted, her voice filled with raw emotion. "It's what I've always done. I always take the safe road. I've never been anywhere. I've never been on an airplane or hiked a mountain or bungee jumped off a ledge. I never challenge anything or anyone. I never say what I really want to say. I always comply. And I never have the courage to say what, or when, or who. All my adult life I've put up with people walking over me, with being overlooked in my work, with my boyfriend taking me for granted… and I've had enough. I want more… I want…"

"You want what?"

Her blue eyes glittered brilliantly. "I want… I want you."

Chapter Ten

It wasn't what she'd expected to say. Or planned. But she was so weary from saying and doing what was expected. In that moment, while he watched her with such profound, heated intensity, Cassie knew exactly what she wanted for the first time in her life. And who. Even if it was simply for one night.

"Cassie, I—"

"Don't say no to me," she implored. "Not tonight."

He didn't move. He looked startled. "You don't know what you're saying."

"I do," she insisted. "I know exactly. Days ago you said you wanted to make love to me."

"And days ago you said it would be a mistake."

He was right. She had said that. Out of fear. And guilt. And some crazy notion that he wanted her out of some kind of cruel revenge. But Tanner wasn't that kind of man. She knew that deep in her heart. "I was wrong to say that to you. It's not what I think. What I feel."

He didn't look convinced. "Sex isn't the answer to erase the pain you're feeling, Cassie. All it will do is confuse us both."

"Maybe I want to be confused," she said and took a step closer, thinking how handsome he looked in his dark suit and tie. "Maybe I want to stop doing what I think I *should* and do what I *want* for a change. And maybe I want to feel something other than grief and sadness. I want to feel heat and sweat and pleasure and—"

"And you'll regret it in the morning," he said, cutting her off.

"So, I'll regret it," she said and shrugged. "I don't care. Isn't it obvious that's exactly my point, Tanner—I don't regret *anything*," she said hotly. "Because I've never done anything to regret. I always take the easy road. I do the right thing. I keep out of trouble. I keep myself protected from really feeling anything."

"Until Doug?"

"Including Doug," she replied. "He was no risk. Because he was never *here*. And even when he was, he always seemed far away and distracted and so completely out of reach. So that made him safe for me, don't you see? It made him easy to be with. My expectations were low and that's all I got."

"You loved him?"

"Yes," she said, and felt so much heat and tension emanating from the man in front of her it was as if a fire had been lit in the room. "Maybe I did. Or maybe I thought I did. Or maybe there's no such thing as love and there's just this…" She stopped and moved in front of him. "Just crazy chemistry and attraction. Just sex."

"Nothing's that simple," he said and swayed toward her.

"Then let's make it simple," she said and placed her palm on his chest. "Stay with me and make love to me tonight."

He moaned as if the idea gave him pain, and for a second she thought he was going to turn away. But he didn't. He reached for her and hauled her against his body, gently fisting a handful of her hair as he tilted her head back.

"And tomorrow?" he asked, his mouth hovering above hers. "What then?"

"I don't want to think about tomorrow. Only now. Only how I want to be with you tonight, without ghosts or pretense between us."

He nodded fractionally and kissed her with such intense passion she almost fainted. When he lifted his mouth from hers she was gasping for breath and so aroused her head was spinning. She pulled back and put space between them, taking in deep gulps of air, her mouth tingling from the heat and passion in his kiss.

She'd never been sexy. She'd never considered herself seductive in any shape or form. And she'd never openly offered herself to anyone in her life. But she'd never wanted a man the way she wanted Tanner, either.

"Cassie...I think—"

"Don't think," she said on a rasp of hot breath. "Don't think about anything except this moment. I don't care about tomorrow and I don't care what this means. Because maybe it doesn't mean anything...maybe it's just about two people who want each other right now." She walked toward the door and looked over her shoulder. "No ghosts," she whispered and then walked down the hallway.

Tanner had imagined and dreamed about being with Cassie more times than he dared count. And in none of those dreams had he let himself believe she'd look at him with such burning, raw desire. She was so incredibly beautiful that he was literally lost for words. Watching her hips sway and the seductive turn of her shoulder as she invited him into her bed was the sexiest thing he'd ever seen in his life.

By the time he'd forced some life into his legs she had disappeared down the hallway. When he reached her bedroom door she was standing at the end of the bed, her eyes clearly saying she was waiting for him. A couple of lit candles flicked shadows on the walls, creating a mood of tempting intimacy.

"No ghosts," she said again, as though she was confirming it one last time.

And Tanner knew there was no wall between them. In that moment, there was only the two of them, together, alone in her bedroom.

But knowing what was about to happen, he gathered his good sense for a second. "Cassie, I'm not exactly prepared for this."

She immediately understood what he meant and walked around the bed. She opened the bedside drawer and extracted a small box. "I am," she said, suddenly all brazen confidence. She dropped a condom on the pillow and moved back around the bed.

She was setting the pace and for the moment he didn't mind one bit.

One hand clasped the top of the coat-style black dress she wore and she began to unclip the buttons with excruciating, seductive slowness. Mesmerized, Tanner stayed by the door and watched, wholly aroused as she popped one button, and then the next, and the next, until the dress was opened right down the front. She shrugged and slipped the garment off her shoulders and it dropped to the floor. The smoothness of her creamy skin was highlighted by the dark contrast of the black bra and briefs she wore, and Tanner clenched his fists to pump some blood back into his hands and heart before he passed out.

The dips and curves of her body were mesmerizing. Her full breasts rounded over the low-cut bra in pure temptation. She twisted her hands behind her back and unclipped her bra. Her breasts fell forward, rosy-tipped and beautiful, and he fought the urge to race forward and take her in a rush of heat and desire. He looked at her breasts and his palms burned with an aching need to touch her. Cassie gave a little smile, as if she knew exactly how enticing she was. She hooked her thumbs into her briefs and pushed them over her hips and past her knees and feet.

There was something ethereally beautiful about her and in all his life he'd never forget how she looked standing naked in front of him—like an entrancing mix of temptation and haunting vulnerability. He wanted to say something. He wanted to tell her how lovely she was and declare every ounce of feeling he had for her. But no words came out. He could only watch, enthralled and aroused, as she met his gaze and smiled.

"Let's have a shower first," she said and backed up until she reached the door of the en suite bathroom.

A shower? Tanner wasn't sure he'd make it. He looked at her, wanting her in ways he hadn't imagined he'd ever want anyone.

But he took about two seconds to ditch his clothes and join her.

She was backed up against the wall and water sluiced over her skin. He hauled her close, kissing her hungrily. She kissed him back and clung to his shoulders. The warm water created an erotic slide between them and he wondered vaguely how he'd ever shower again without imagining, without wanting Cassie pressed against him.

She said his name low in her throat and Tanner eased back. She looked up and smiled as she grabbed the soap, put a little space between them and slowly worked the bar over his chest in small circles into a foamy lather. Tanner dropped his arms to his sides and clenched his fists. He'd let her have her way for the moment. Besides, with all the blood rushing to one part of his body he actually wondered if he might really pass out. She toyed with his nipples for a second and smiled.

"You're smiling?"

She met his gaze. "You make me smile. You make me…"

"What?" he prompted, then took the soap from her hand and dropped it back into the dish.

"Confident," she admitted huskily. "Unafraid."

"I'm glad. And you are those things, Cassie. You're strong and beautiful and smart."

She sighed, and the sound echoed through his chest. Then he kissed her, hotly, hungrily, taking her tongue in an erotic dance. She kissed him back. He kissed her again. Back and forth, taking and giving.

"Cassandra," he muttered against her lips. "Let's get out of here."

She nodded and he switched off the water. They were out of the shower in seconds and dried off just as quickly. By the time they tumbled onto the bed Tanner had captured her mouth again and kissed her long and deep. She lay down and he moved to her side. He ran his fingertips over her hip and waist before gently grazing his knuckles against one erect nipple. She moaned and raised her mouth to his again, kissing him sweetly. Tanner cupped her breasts, first one, and then the other, before he replaced his hands with his mouth. Cassie arched back on the bed as he rolled his tongue across the tender flesh.

They kissed and touched, fuelling the heat swirling between them. Each stroke was hotter than the one before, each kiss deeper. Every sigh she gave made Tanner want to love her more, need her more, as if he needed air in his lungs.

Her hands were over his chest, his ribs and his waist. There was nothing shy about her touch. When she reached lower and touched him where he ached to be touched, Tanner thought he might pass out. He ran his hands along her skin, finding the place where she was wet and ready for him, and slowly caressed her, finding a gentle rhythm that made her moan encouragingly. Tanner watched her come apart in his arms and felt her pleasure across his skin and through his blood.

"Now," she whispered breathlessly against his mouth and linked her leg through his. "Please."

Tanner speedily retrieved the condom from the pillow. She took it and sheathed him quickly. And when finally he was inside her, looking down into her beautiful face, he could think only one thing.

I'm home...

Cassie knew making love with Tanner would be extraordinary. She knew his touch would drive her wild. But she hadn't expected that his possession would consume her mind, her body and her heart. He rested his weight on his arms as they moved together and she was eased into a rhythm that created a heady sensation of narcotic pleasure that pulsed through her blood. With each smooth stroke she was drawn higher. With each kiss she was pushed toward the edge. She touched his shoulders, his arms, his back. She pressed her palms and fingers into his skin to get closer, to feel every inch of him against her. As their kisses grew more urgent, heat spread through her body like wildfire. Cassie felt Tanner tense above her and she instinctively wrapped her legs around him, drawing him closer, wanting him deeper, until they were both taken by a rush of white-hot, incandescent pleasure that left her breathless and more connected to him than she'd ever been to another person in her whole life.

When he rolled onto his back, drawing deep breaths into his lungs, Cassie felt the loss of his skin against hers as if she'd lost part of herself. He grabbed her hand and gently kissed her knuckles.

"Be back in a minute," he said. He got up and disappeared into the bathroom.

Cassie stretched and sighed. She'd never made love with such passion. Never been so in tune with a lover that it was as though they had been together in another life. Somehow, he knew her. He knew where to touch, where to stroke, where to kiss with a kind of instinctual, soul-reaching intensity.

Is this love?

It didn't feel like any kind of love she'd experienced before. Because there was a deep connection between them. They'd become friends and now lovers. And it had left her forever changed. When he returned she'd rolled onto her side and he slipped back onto the bed and lay beside her.

"Are you okay?" he asked softly.

She sighed and smiled. "Yes. I'm…good."

His eyes darkened and he traced the back of his fingers over her shoulder and waist and then laid his hand on her hip. "That was…something."

Cassie's mouth curved with delight. She'd never had such a lovely compliment. "Yes, it was." She ran her hand along his biceps and fingered the hard muscle. "You know, you have a remarkable body."

Laughter rumbled in his chest. "You, too." He moved

his hand to her cheek and kissed her tenderly. "Your lips taste so good."

She smiled against his mouth, and then trailed kisses down his neck and lingered at the base of his throat, where his pulse beat strongly. "You taste good, too," she whispered and moved lower. "Like here," she teased and moved lower again, sliding her lips down his chest. "And here."

Tanner groaned as his arms came around her and he pulled her close. He grasped her chin, tilted her face back to meet his and kissed her deeply. They made love again, this time it was slow and languorous as he trailed his mouth down her body and then back up again. He kissed her breasts, her rib cage, her belly and lower still, sending her spinning into a vortex of pleasure so intense, so agonizingly intimate, she could barely draw breath into her lungs as she came apart in his arms.

"Does it hurt?" she asked much later as she lay against his chest and trailed a finger over the long scar on his left thigh.

"Sometimes," he said as he grabbed her hand and laid it against his stomach.

"You could have been killed in that accident."

"But I wasn't," he said and caressed her back. "I'm here. With you."

She smiled against his chest. "I'm glad." She sighed. "By the way, I kind of like you calling me Cassandra."

Tanner chuckled softly. "Then I will," he said and stroked her skin. "In moments like this one."

She nodded and smiled at how intimate that sounded. "What time is it?"

He shifted a little to check the clock on the bedside table. "Just after ten."

She stirred. "Oliver will wake up in about an hour for a feed. And I'm hungry."

"Me, too," he said and rolled her onto her back effortlessly as he kissed her. "Let's go and eat some leftovers."

She nodded. Once he released her Cassie slid off the mattress and grabbed her robe from the end of the bed. Tanner was sitting up, watching her.

"What?" she asked.

He shrugged and grinned. "Nothing. I like looking at you."

Cassie smiled. "You mean you like looking at me naked?"

"Well...yeah. But I like looking at you in any way. I like watching you with Oliver. I like watching you sleep." He grinned. "Even though you snore."

She stopped tying the sash on her robe and laughed. "I do not."

"You do," he insisted, still grinning.

She popped her hands on her hips. "And when have you seen me sleep?"

"When you were sick," he replied and pointed to the chair in the corner. "I sat there for a while."

Cassie stilled. "That was you? I sensed someone was in the room. I thought it was Lauren."

He shook his head. "I didn't want to leave you alone in case you needed something."

Cassie's heart flipped over. "That was very sweet of you. You've done so much for me. I don't feel like I've done anything in return."

One dark brow came up and he glanced at the rumpled bedsheets. "No?"

Color spotted her cheeks. "Well, besides what we just did before. I'm not sure that counts."

He laughed softly and sprang off the bed, coming around to take her in his arms. "Oh, sweetheart," he said and drew her close as his hands slipped beneath the robe to caress her skin. "That counts… That definitely counts."

And for the next half hour her only thoughts were of the man who'd possessed her body and captured her heart.

When Tanner rolled out of bed the following morning it was past seven. The sheets beside him were cool, so he figured Cassie must have been awake for some time. They'd been up a couple of times during the night to tend to a restless Oliver, before heading back to bed to make lazy love again before dawn broke.

He stood, stretched and grabbed the trousers and briefs he'd dumped at the end of the bed in such a hurry the night before. His leg ached and he pressed a hand to the fracture line. He really needed to get back to physical therapy when he returned to Cedar Creek.

But the mere thought of the idea made his chest hurt.

He zipped up the trousers and stretched his shoulders out a little more. He needed coffee and food. Cassie was in the kitchen when he walked through the door, feeding Oliver and laughing with her son. She looked up and smiled.

"Good morning," she said.

It was a good morning. The best of his life. She looked so adorable in her soft pink robe with the baby in her lap, and as Tanner watched them a deep surge of unquestionable love washed over him. It was unlike any other feeling he'd ever known. And he knew he wanted them for his own. The woman he loved and the son she'd borne to another man. His brother's family. The family Doug had intended to discard.

"What are you thinking about?" she asked, still smiling.

Tanner returned the gesture. "How beautiful you look in the morning." He walked to the table and held out his hands to take the baby.

Once Oliver was settled in his arms she got up and poured coffee for them both.

"You're so good with him," she said, smiling as she brought the mugs to the table. "You really are a natural with babies. I was so unsure and awkward with him when I first brought him home. I'm a little envious."

Tanner grinned as Oliver grabbed one of his fingers and held on. "He's easy to love."

"He's going to miss you when you leave," she said on a sigh, and the mood in the room altered immediately. "So am I."

Tanner looked up and met her gaze, his insides aching. "I can't stay, Cassie."

She nodded. "I know. And I don't mean to make you feel obligated to stay or anything like that. I'm just…" She stopped and patted her heart with her palm. "I'm just saying what's in here."

Tanner pushed back the swell of emotion rising in his throat. What was she really saying? That she had feelings for him? He knew that. Two people didn't make love as they had and *not* have feelings for each other. But he wasn't about to kid himself into thinking it meant she'd fallen in love with him. She'd loved Doug. She probably still did. But last night she'd been grieving and sad and needed someone. Probably anyone. And he'd been there for her. That's all it was.

"I told you making love would complicate things."

She shrugged a little. "And I told you I didn't care. I still don't. I'm glad we had last night. It was…lovely. And I'll never regret it."

He should have been pleased. But inside, he hurt all over. If she'd had regrets it would have been a whole lot easier to leave her as he knew he had to. He needed to return to South Dakota. But the very notion of leaving her and Oliver made his bones ache.

"Neither will I," he said and knew it was a lie. Tanner did regret it. Because he knew it wouldn't happen again. She wasn't his to love. Or have.

"Would you tell me about Leah?"

Leah? He hadn't expected that. Tanner looked at her directly. "Why?"

"I'd like to know what happened...how two very different brothers could love the same woman."

Oh...God. Tanner inwardly groaned. *If she only knew.*

"We met in high school and dated for a while."

"You were serious about her?" Cassie asked. "You loved her?"

He shrugged. "I thought so at the time."

"And then Doug came along?"

"Something like that," he said, ignoring the jabs of unease crawling across his skin. "She fell for him and they had an affair."

"Behind your back?"

"I wouldn't have kept seeing her had I known," he said drily. "When she found out she was pregnant she came clean and told me Doug was the father."

Cassie's face screwed up. "You must have been devastated."

"Well, it wasn't exactly a picnic. But I could see how upset and sorry she was. And eventually I got through it."

"Is that when you started traveling? I remember Doug telling me how you took off when you were eighteen. He said you wanted to get away from Crystal Point. He said you hated the town and everything in it. But that's not true," she said, watching him over the rim of her mug. "It was him you wanted to get away from. And the memories."

"I guess," Tanner said, rocking Oliver gently. "Even

though Doug didn't live here, we'd always stay with Ruthie when we came back to town. I had plans to buy a place around here. Maybe a small cane farm or enough land to graze cattle. But the money was gone and Leah was gone, too…so I took off. I backpacked through Asia and then traveled through Europe for a while. When I was twenty Ruthie arranged for me to spend a summer on her brother-in-law's horse ranch in Cedar Creek. And I've been there ever since. I worked at a few different ranches around the county, breaking and training horses, and saved enough to finally get my own place a couple of years back."

Cassie's eyes glistened. "So had things been different, you might have stayed here. You might have bought a place close by and been a part of this town. And we might have met before I—"

"Before you met Doug, you mean?" Tanner shrugged one shoulder. "But we did meet, remember? When we were thirteen."

She nodded. "I know we did. I guess I was thinking about before Doug bought this house. When you came here that first time to visit Doug…did you remember me?"

"Yes."

"We didn't talk much that visit," she said. "At the time I'd wondered if you thought I wasn't right…you know… for your brother."

Tanner met her gaze. "I only thought, how did he get so lucky."

She smiled. "That's sweet. But now that I know you I feel very foolish for believing him so unconditionally."

"You trusted him. You had no reason not to."

"I suppose. He was a complex man and I don't think I ever really knew that until now."

Tanner could see the sadness in her expression and lifted Oliver toward her. "He's all that matters, right?"

She smiled and her eyes brightened. "Absolutely."

"Let's do something today," he suggested. "I promised Ruthie I'd work with her colt this morning, but later we could go out…maybe have lunch in town?"

She nodded and accepted Oliver in her arms. "We might even persuade Ruthie to join us," she said. "A family outing would be great."

A family outing…

Doug's family. And nothing would ever change that.

Chapter Eleven

"So, something's clearly changed between the two of you. That girl can hardly keep her eyes off you today."

Tanner strapped the girth tightly around the colt and ignored the comment. He'd made the mistake of bringing Cassie and Oliver to the Nevelson farm, allowing them to all be scrutinized by a very discerning and curious Ruthie.

"I reckon one more long reining session should do it," he said and checked the bit and bridle. "Then he should be ready to back with the saddle and ride."

Ruthie ducked through the fence. "Don't think you're getting away from me that easily."

He stilled and looked at her. "No comment."

She tutted. "Not like you to let that part of your anatomy do your thinking," she said bluntly. "Just be careful."

"I'm always careful," he said and clicked the colt to step backward. It was the truth. When it came to love and sex Tanner had been cautious and careful his whole life. He'd never let himself get too close... He'd never lasted longer than a few months in any relationship.

"You're in love with her," Ruthie said so matter-of-factly that Tanner stopped what he was doing and faced her.

"That would be foolish."

"Yes," she agreed and nodded. "It would be. And you've never been a foolish man. Until now." She crossed her bony arms and frowned. "Next thing I know you'll be asking her to go back to South Dakota and marry you."

Tanner's body turned rigid. "No one's business," he said and quickly got back to the task. He wasn't about to admit that the thought had crossed his mind more than once that morning. Being with Cassie and Oliver was like nothing he'd ever experienced before. For the first time in his life he was exactly where he wanted to be. And with whom he wanted. And as much as he knew the whole situation was a complicated mess, he didn't want that to end.

"I like Cassie. She's a sweet girl and was always too good for your brother. But he'll always be between you," Ruthie said, the ever frank voice of reason. "As much as you don't want him to be. As much as you try to ignore it."

Doug...

Most of his life Tanner had gone from loving, to hating, to resenting his brother. But he'd never envied Doug or wanted anything his brother had. Until the day he was introduced to Cassie. It had taken about two seconds to realize she was the same girl he'd kissed on the beach all those years before. Doug had told him she was compliant and uncomplicated and undemanding—exactly the kind of woman his brother was attracted to—one who wouldn't challenge him or ask anything of Doug he wasn't prepared to give. And Cassie, with her sweet demeanor and haunting vulnerability, was an easy target for his charming, often misguided brother.

But when she told Doug she was pregnant and wanted a commitment his brother had done exactly what Tanner would have expected…he'd retreated into his soldier shell and told her they'd discuss it when he returned from tour. All the while planning on abandoning her and the baby if she chose to continue with her pregnancy. Just as he had with Leah.

"I know what I'm doing," he said and led the colt around the corral.

Ruthie followed, unperturbed by his brush-off. "I hope so. And remember, once you tell her how you feel there's no taking it back."

He was still thinking about Ruthie's words half an hour later as he dumped the long-reining gear back to the small tack room at the end of the stables. Ruthie was right. There was no taking it back. Which was exactly why he hadn't said it. He *was* in love with Cassie. He loved Cassie *and* Oliver and ached to make them his own. But he wasn't in the market for a rejection. And while Cassie had hinted that she had feelings for him other than the attraction that had landed them in bed together, he couldn't be sure.

"You know, there's something sexy about watching a man work with a horse."

He turned. Cassie stood in the narrow doorway. In jeans and a bright red shirt she looked so dazzling it stole his breath. "Have you been watching from the house?"

"I may have admired you from the kitchen window once or twice." She stepped into the small room. "What were you and Ruthie talking about?" she asked and grinned. "Me?" She chuckled and the lovely sound hit him directly behind the ribs. "I think she's onto us."

"Yeah," Tanner said and managed a tight smile as he shifted a couple of saddles onto a rack. "She doesn't miss much."

Cassie came closer and sat on a hay bale. "Everything okay?"

"Sure. Is Oliver asleep?"

"Yes. Ruthie's watching him." Her mouth curved. "So I thought I'd come and keep you company for a while. I was also thinking of turning over a new leaf...you know, like start trying new things."

Tanner's hands stilled on a saddle. "New things?" he queried.

"Well, I've never been on an airplane, so that's something I'd like to do at some point. And I thought I might like to learn how to ride a horse," she said and smiled suggestively. "If I can find someone to teach me."

Tanner's stomach was in knots. They both knew there wasn't time for that. He was leaving in a week or so. But he smiled agreeably. "Ruthie's got an old gelding down the back pasture that would do well enough."

"Great," she said and got to her feet. She came close and touched his arm. "We should probably get going if we're to have our outing this afternoon."

"Sure," he said and grasped her hand. "I need to clean up first. Let me finish up here and I'll meet you in the house."

"Okay," she said and stretched on her toes to kiss him.

Tanner wrapped his arms around her and returned the kiss. They remained in the tack room for a few minutes, making out, kissing and touching as if they hadn't a care in the world. When they finally pulled apart he was aroused and unable to hide the fact.

"Ah—Cassie, we'd better stop."

She smiled, as though she knew exactly what she'd done to him. "See you soon," she said and walked off.

By the time he returned to the house, showered and changed it was past one o'clock. Ruthie declined their in-

vitation to join them and waved them off as they headed
off down the driveway. Oliver was gurgling happily in his
baby seat. Cassie was humming to an old song on the radio.
In that moment he had everything he wanted.

The Mount Merry Animal Haven was half an hour outside of Bellandale and had always been one of Cassie's favorite places as a child. She was delighted when Tanner
suggested they visit. It had been a home and sanctuary
for animals in need for decades and while the proprietors
had changed hands, the peacefulness and serenity of the
place had remained unchanged. With Oliver in his stroller
and Tanner by her side, they walked around the farm in
the afternoon sunshine and Cassie experienced something
she'd long forgotten but always longed for.

Family...

As she had when her parents were alive. Or when her
grandfather had taken her in and made a home for her.
She'd buried her grandfather the day before and today
could have been a sad, terrible day. But Tanner had made
sure she wasn't alone. He'd taken her to Ruthie's and in-
cluded her in his day. Being with him and Oliver took her
mind off losing her grandfather and even if it was just for
that moment, she'd treasure the memory forever.

After they visited the baby animal yard and patted an
ornery mule whose name was Duke, they had lunch in
the small teahouse on the property. For the next hour they
chatted to the owners about the animals and laughed when
they shared stories about the two ill-mannered llamas that
had recently been re-homed with them.

Tanner was attentive and charming and so easy to be
around that with each passing hour, she fell for him just
that little bit more. Had she ever been so comfortable

around anyone before? Had anyone ever made her feel so at ease and so happy in her own skin?

No. It was a startling realization. For the past few years she'd believed Doug was the kind of man she wanted. But she'd been so wrong. Even though Tanner was a little bossy and sometimes showed an arrogant streak, he possessed such elemental goodness that it was impossible to *not* be drawn toward him.

But he's leaving...remember?

The idea of losing him from her life was heart-wrenching. He hadn't spoken about his impending departure and she hadn't raised the subject, either. Because her heart didn't want to hear it. She didn't want to lose him. Even though she knew it was inevitable. The house was for sale, she needed to find a new home and Tanner was going back to South Dakota.

Accept it...there's no changing the inevitable.

Or was there?

All her life she'd accepted things. Without argument. Without resistance. Hadn't she blindly accepted her mediocre relationship with Doug? As if it was all she deserved? His brief visits and lack of commitment should have sent warning bells screaming off in her head. But instead she'd simply acquiesced and accepted it. When she'd told him she was pregnant he'd fobbed her off and said they'd talk soon. On his terms. Not hers. Even when she knew she deserved better. But she wasn't that woman anymore. Tanner had shown her that. He'd somehow given her the gumption she'd been lacking most of her life.

After lunch they had photographs taken with a bald parrot named George who wore a tiny crocheted jacket and nibbled on Cassie's earlobe. Tanner bought Oliver a T-shirt from the gift shop and chatted to the elderly sales assistant behind the counter, who they quickly discovered was the aunt of the owner and volunteered in the shop on the weekends.

The older woman came around the counter and peered into the stroller. "He's such a beautiful baby, such gorgeous big brown eyes," she remarked and smiled. "You must feel very blessed." She looked at Oliver again, then Tanner, and met Cassie's gaze. "And goodness, doesn't he look the spitting image of his daddy."

For a second the silence was deafening. Cassie knew she should have corrected the other woman. But nothing came out. Tanner remained standing by the stroller, silent and unmoving. Of course it was a natural assumption. They were together. They had a baby with them. Anyone who didn't know them would come to the same conclusion and think the baby was theirs. It shouldn't have made her feel uncomfortable. But it did. She looked at Tanner and tried to read his expression. But his face was a handsome, impassive mask. Of course he wouldn't want people to assume that another man's child was his. Oliver was Doug's son. One day, Tanner would have his own family. His own child. And Oliver would be the nephew he saw occasionally.

And I'll be forgotten.

It hurt to think it. But she had to stop silly dreams from taking over. Tanner wanted his own family. Not his brother's leftovers. They'd had the discussion a week earlier and he hadn't denied it. And she didn't blame him. She couldn't. He probably regretted last night, too. He'd warned her how sex would complicate things and he was right on the money. She'd allowed her loneliness and her libido to take control.

They left around four o'clock and headed back to Crystal Point. Tanner was quiet on the drive home and with

Oliver sleeping soundly in the backseat and the radio off, the only sound was the gentle hum of the engine.

"Everything okay?" she asked.

"Of course."

She wasn't entirely convinced. "It was a nice afternoon."

"Yes," he said and glanced over his shoulder to Oliver. "But I think we wore him out."

"He'll sleep well tonight," she said and fought the urge to lay a hand on Tanner's jeans-clad thigh. His touch was like tonic and she wanted to feel it again. She wanted to be swept away by his kiss and feel the ecstasy of his complete possession. She wanted him in her bed. She just wasn't sure if that's what he wanted, too. "So…are you staying for dinner tonight?"

"Am I invited?" he asked, looking at the road ahead.

"Of course."

He looked sideways for a moment. "Okay."

There was an elephant in the room. Or more to the point, in the car. And Cassie figured out what it was quick smart.

"You don't have to stay the night, Tanner," she said and crossed her hands tightly in her lap. "I'm not going to jump you like I did last night, if that's what's on your mind."

She saw a smile crease his mouth.

"You're not?" he queried. "Too bad for me, then."

He was impossible to read and Cassie's temperature rose a little. "So, you want to stay?" she asked, suddenly annoyed. "Is that what you're saying?"

"Of course I want to stay," he replied tensely.

"Could have fooled me," she muttered and looked out the side window.

"What?"

She shook her head. "Nothing."

He was staying. *Great.* She should have been happy. It's what she wanted. Another night in his arms. Another night tasting his kisses and feeling the tenderness of his touch. But she was angry instead.

By the time he pulled the car into the driveway she was so annoyed her skin was hot all over. She grabbed Oliver's bag and her tote and waited for Tanner to get the stroller from the car before she hiked up the path to the door and unlocked the house. Tanner followed behind her and met her in the nursery. She held out her arms and took the baby.

"Thank you. I'm going to get him bathed and fed."

Mouse barked and Tanner nodded. "I'll feed the dog."

"Okay," she said stiffly and waited for him to leave the room before she took another breath. She hugged Oliver close and felt some of her rage disappear. She loved her son with all her heart. And he was her only priority.

She bathed him, dressed him in his pajamas, then went to the kitchen and made up his bottle. Determined to avoid Tanner for the moment, she returned to the nursery to feed her son and stayed another half an hour until he drifted off to sleep.

By the time she was back in the kitchen it was nearly six o'clock. She grabbed the kettle to make tea and only stopped when she heard Tanner moving in the doorway.

"Is he asleep?" he asked.

"Yes," she replied, not looking at him. "Do you want tea? Coffee?"

"Coffee," he said and came behind the counter. "But I'll do it. You make lousy coffee."

Cassie turned and glared at him. "I do not."

"Oh, yeah, you do."

She popped a tea bag in her mug and slid another mug along the counter. "Fine. Suit yourself."

Since she was trapped in the kitchen and couldn't get

past without pressing close to him, Cassie stayed where she was. He made coffee as effortlessly as he did most things, which only amplified her irritation. She crossed her arms, raised her chin and stared at the ceiling.

"You're not going to slug me again, are you?" he asked, resting back on the countertop, coffee in hand.

Her eyes flashed in his direction. "You're such a jerk."

"And you've got a bad temper."

"Around you?" she countered. "Yeah. And while we're on the subject of my faults, I'm sorry about what the lady said in the shop. I should have corrected her."

He straightened and placed the mug on the counter with deliberate emphasis. "Why?" he asked quietly. "Because you can't bear the thought of Oliver being anyone else's but Doug's?"

He sounded offended. And mad. Cassie looked at him. "No, I just didn't think you'd want—"

"If you must know, I wish he *was* mine," he said, harsher than she'd ever heard.

Did she just hear him right? *Oh, God...I wish that, too...*

"You...you do?" she stammered.

He nodded and she saw the pulse in his cheek throb. "It sure would make this mess a hell of a lot less complicated."

"Mess?" she echoed. "That's what we are to you?"

He sighed impatiently. "Don't play with my words. That's not what I meant and you know it."

Cassie flapped her hands. "I don't know anything when it comes to you. You're...you're...impossible to read. Impossible to get close to." When his brows came up she planted her hands on her hips. "And I don't mean in bed. If communicating with you was as simple as sex, then we'd obviously be fine."

"Then perhaps that's what we should do?" he suggested and placed an arm either side of her as he leaned closer.

"Forget the arguing. Forget the talking. Forget everything but this."

She looked up, mesmerized by the dark passion in his eyes and the intent in his expression. And she wanted him. She wanted him so much she ached.

He kissed her, long and hard and so intense it had possession stamped all over it.

And of course she kissed him back. It was pure instinct. Pure longing. Pure, unadulterated desire for his touch that drove her beyond coherent thought. His tongue found hers as his hands roamed down her back and he lifted her up, holding her against him intimately as their mouths melded together. Cassie gripped his shoulders and wrapped her legs around his waist as he walked backward.

They made it to her bedroom in record time and their clothes came off just as quickly.

It was hot and quick and explosive. There was no finesse this time, no tender touch. Cassie came apart in his arms, begging for him to possess her and he took her on a wild, heavenly ride that she never wanted to end. She told him what she wanted and he did the same. She said words she'd never spoken to another person. She demanded. She complied. She gave herself up and offered all she could give in return. There was no going back. No way to retreat. They were in that one perfect moment, completely in tune. As the pleasure built she gripped him hard, holding on, feeling every ounce of his need for her and hers for him. Until finally they were thrown over the edge and rode the waves of an earth-shattering climax.

When it was over they both dropped back onto the bed, breathless and stunned by the intensity of what they'd just shared. She'd never behaved like that before. Never begged. Never moaned and writhed and been so completely out of control. Her entire body pulsed in the aftermath. And all she could think was how she wanted to make love with him again. And again. He was her lover. The only one who mattered. The only one she wanted.

And then Tanner said four words that brought her back to reality with a thud.

"We didn't use protection."

Cassie stilled. No. They hadn't. She did the math in her head and figured there was very little risk. "I'm sure it's fine."

"That was irresponsible of me. I'm sorry."

"My fault, too," she said a little irritably, thinking he had no right to shoulder all the responsibility.

He was still breathing hard and Cassie watched his chest rise up and down. She wanted to touch him again. She wanted to feel him over her and inside her. She didn't want to talk about what might be. Although the notion of having his baby filled her entire body with a heady warmth.

"You'd tell me, wouldn't you?"

She ignored her breathlessness and sat up. "What?"

"If something happened...you'd tell me?"

"Do you mean would I tell you if I were pregnant?" She twisted around to face him. "Of course I would. But there's not much chance."

"Would you mind?" he asked. "I mean, if it did happen?"

"Would I mind having two kids under two years of age?" She laughed lightly. "Piece of cake. But since there's little chance it will happen, I'm not going to get worked up about it." She reached out and traced her fingertips along his rib cage and he quickly grabbed her hand. "You really do want children, though? I mean, one day?"

He entwined their fingers. "Definitely."

"You'll make a good dad," she said, ignoring the twinges inside. He would make a great dad. The best.

And she wished…she wished that Oliver would one day have a father like him.

I wish Oliver had Tanner for a father.

And there it was. Exactly what she wanted. She wanted Tanner. Because…because she was in love with him. Wholly and completely. He'd captured her heart with his kindness and goodness. He was what she'd secretly dreamed of all her life.

"I wish… I wish he was your son, too," she said, so quietly she wondered if he'd heard.

Tanner didn't move. Didn't say anything. An uneasy silence filled the room. Something was wrong.

Finally he released her hand and sat up, swinging his legs off the bed. And still he stayed silent. He grabbed his jeans from the floor and stood as he slipped them back on. Cassie watched, fascinated and confused, motionless as he left the room without looking at her. Or saying a word.

I said the wrong thing…

She pulled her knees up and hugged them.

What do I do now?

Hadn't she just bared herself to him? Didn't he know what her words meant?

She shimmied off the bed and looked for her clothes. She found some gray sweats in a pile of freshly washed and folded clothes she'd laid on the chair in the corner and snatched them up quickly. Once she was dressed she walked down the hallway. She checked on Oliver and then headed for the living room.

Tanner was standing by the window, his jeans low on his hips, his chest bare. Looking at him made her breath catch in her throat and he turned at the sound.

"Are you okay?"

He nodded, but he looked tense, as if he had a heavy weight pressing down on his shoulders.

"I'm sorry if I said something I shouldn't have," she said and stepped into the room. "I'm so confused at the moment all I can do is—"

"I could be."

Cassie stilled as the air caught in her lungs. "What?"

"I could be Oliver's father."

She shuddered. What was he saying? "I don't understand what you mean."

But with his next words she understood. And it rocked her to the core.

"Marry me."

Chapter Twelve

She looked stunned. And she looked as though she thought he'd lost his mind. Which, considering he'd just proposed marriage to the woman who had loved his brother and probably still did, he clearly had.

"You're not serious?"

"Perfectly."

"But we hardly…" Her words trailed off. "That's crazy."

"Not really," he said and sat down on the sofa. "Oliver needs a father. He's my nephew and I love him. And you and I are… We're good together."

"Good in bed, you mean?"

"I mean good together," he said again. "We work. We have a lot in common. We get along. And yeah, we're great in bed together. It's a starting point, Cassie. And more than what some people ever get."

And I love you…

But he didn't say it. The words stuck on the edge of his

tongue and if he thought he had a hope that she loved him, too, he would have said them. Maybe over time. Maybe once they were married and had more children together. Maybe she'd forget she'd loved Doug before him.

She moved farther into the room and sank into a chair. "But marriage? I mean, there's so much to consider. For starters, where would we live?"

"South Dakota."

Her eyes grew wide. "You're asking me to move to South Dakota? With Oliver? Just like that?"

"What's keeping you here?" he asked. "This house? It's being sold. Family? Oliver is your family. There's nothing really keeping you here now, is there? Your grandfather's gone. Doug's gone. And I don't mean to hurt you by saying that."

"But I have friends who—"

"I'm your friend, Cassie," he said quietly. "And I'm asking you to be more than that. I'm asking to be your husband."

She was visibly shaking. Shocked. Maybe appalled. He couldn't tell. He wanted to rush over and take her in his arms and tell her everything would be okay. He wanted to assure her that he'd care for her and Oliver forever. That she could rely on him. Trust him.

He waited, hoping she'd come to see it was the most sensible option. The best thing for Oliver. And them. But she didn't say a word. She stared into her lap, hands linked.

"Cassie?"

She took a breath and looked up. The emotion in her eyes couldn't be disguised. "I don't know… I feel a little overwhelmed by this. It's all happened so fast."

"And you need time to think it over?" he suggested.

She nodded. "Yes. For Oliver's sake."

"Then I'll stay as long as you need." He came across the

room and sat beside her, taking her hands gently within his. "I know you're scared, Cassie. I know this might seem like it's come way out of left field. But think about it sensibly... We both want what's best for Oliver. And I..." He stopped, squeezing her hands. "I care about you both. And I want him to know family and to have what we both missed out on. And we can give him that...you and me. We can make the kind of life together that was taken from us when we were kids."

Tears glittered in her blue eyes. "But if we got married you'd be stuck with us and—"

"That's the whole point, Cassie," he said and drew her hands toward his chest. "I want to be stuck with you. To you. I want to be the person you rely on. I want to be there for you, Cassie. I know this is the right thing to do," he said and tapped his chest with their linked hands. "I feel it in here."

She shuddered and exhaled heavily. "I need... I need some time to think about it."

"Of course," he said and stroked her hair. "I'll give you all the time you need."

She met his gaze and smiled tremulously. "The thing is...I don't want to take advantage of you. I couldn't live with myself if I thought I was doing that. I know you're doing this for Oliver and—"

"I'm doing this for me," he assured her and smiled. "Selfishly, I might add."

She shook her head. "You're the most *unselfish* person I've ever met, Tanner. And I know logic is on your side and I'm probably being typically overcautious and afraid...but this is a huge step and one neither of us can take lightly."

"We won't," he said firmly. "Take some time to think it over. Take a few days. I'll still be here. Call me when you've made a decision." He dropped her hands and got to his feet. "This is the right thing to do, Cassie. For all of us."

He stared down at her, hating to leave, but knowing she needed some time alone.

And then he left.

"Are you considering it?"

Cassie looked across the table at her friends. Lauren and M.J. had arrived an hour earlier for an emergency Monday-night meeting. She'd had thirty-six hours to think about Tanner's proposal and was as confused as ever.

Lauren's question hung in the air. Was she? She said yes a hundred times in her mind. Until a tiny voice of reason had talked her out of it again and again.

"I don't know."

M.J. got more to the point. "But you're sleeping with him, right?"

"Well...we've been together...yes."

"And you're in love with him?"

Her skin heated. "I...I think so..."

M.J.'s dramatic brows came up high. "So, you're lovers and you *think* you love him and he's great with Oliver and he wants to marry you and take you to live on his ranch in South Dakota. What's the problem?"

"Me," she replied with a sob. "*I'm* the problem."

"Is this about Doug?" Lauren asked gently.

Doug? Had she spared the other man a thought for the past two days? Not exactly. His memory had faded in and out. Her head was filled with Tanner and little else. But maybe, in her deepest heart, it was about Doug. Maybe all her reluctance stemmed from the man she'd once thought she'd loved.

"I'm not sure," she said and sighed as she pointed to her temple. "I know in here that marrying Tanner makes perfect sense. But in my heart I feel as though I'm cheating. I know Tanner adores Oliver and wants to do what's best for him. And what he said about us both losing our families when we were young and how now we can make sure that doesn't happen to my son…that makes sense, too. But, is it selfish of me to take that dream? Being with Tanner is easy. Oh, don't get me wrong, he makes me mad and drives me crazy at times…but we have this incredible connection that I've never felt before. But I know Tanner's feelings aren't the same. He loves Oliver and for the moment he wants me…because I'm here and I'm Oliver's mother and it's logical for him to take us both. But he also wants to find that one great love and I know that couldn't possibly be me…not with our history…not with Doug's memory in the background. So I'm scared. I'm scared of letting him go and not ever feeling this again. I'm also scared that one day in the future Tanner will wake up and realize he's made a huge mistake."

"I get what you're saying," M.J. offered a little more gently than usual. "But I don't think it's up to you to stop Tanner from making a mistake."

Her friend was right and Cassie knew one thing. She had a decision to make.

And fast.

On Tuesday morning Cassie was getting Oliver dressed when her phone rang. It was Doug's lawyer. She'd spoken to him a couple of times over the past few months when she'd made tentative inquiries about Doug's estate. But this was the first time he'd called her. She gripped the handset, took a breath and listened to the deep voice on the other end of the phone.

And by the time the call ended Cassie felt as if her heart was suddenly wrapped in stone.

She'd called. And Tanner was foolishly hopeful she'd come to a decision. He hadn't seen Cassie or Oliver for days and he was eager to spend time with them both. He pulled the car into her driveway around seven, got out and walked to her porch.

She met him at the door and opened the screen. She looked tired, he noticed, and a little pale. And then he figured she'd probably gotten as much sleep as he had during the past few days. He moved to kiss her but she ducked away and headed for the living room.

Okay…not exactly the greeting he'd hoped for. He'd been walking around on autopilot for days, wondering, hoping…but never letting himself get accustomed to the idea that she would accept his marriage proposal.

"Is Oliver asleep?" he asked when they reached the front room.

She was by the window, arms crossed and her expression distant. "Yes."

"I've missed him," he said and smiled. "I've missed you."

"Really?"

Tanner stepped around the sofa. Something was wrong. "Cassie, I—"

"Where's my letter?"

He came to an abrupt halt about five feet from her. "What?"

"My letter," she said again, unmoving. "From Doug."

Tanner's blood ran cold. "How did you—"

"The lawyer rang me today. I guess he wanted to dot the *i*'s and cross the *t*'s before the file is closed. And he asked if I'd received the letter from Doug. The one that was in the safety deposit box. The safety deposit box you said was empty. You know, *my letter*."

"Cassie," he said quietly. "I can explain."

"Explain?" she echoed. "Are you serious? I don't want an explanation, Tanner. I just want the letter."

CLAIMING HIS BROTHER'S BABY

His chest tightened. "No, you don't.'

She crossed the floor in a couple of strides and stood in front of him. "I want it. I want to read it. I want to know what's in it. I want to know what Doug had to say to me before he headed into some covert, secret military operation that ended up killing him. I want to know what his last thoughts to me were."

"No," he said again, firmer this time. "You don't."

Her eyes were huge in her face. "Why are you being like this? You've obviously read it… What's in it that makes you think I wouldn't want to read it, too?"

"You need to trust me."

She shook her head. "I don't *need* to do any such thing. And right in this moment, trusting you is the last thing on my mind."

He didn't move. "This is for the best, Cassie."

She glared at him. "You arrogant jerk! You had no right to keep something like this from me."

"I know you're upset," he said, refusing to comply. "But I did it *for* you, Cassie…not to distress you."

"I don't care," she said angrily. "You don't get to decide what's best for me." She sucked in a long breath. "Where is it?" she demanded.

"I destroyed it."

She shuddered visibly. "How could you do that? You had no right."

Tanner braced his hands on his hips and exhaled heavily. "I did what I had to do."

"It wasn't your decision to—"

"Actually," he said, cutting her off, "it was. Doug left the contents of the safety deposit box to me, and that gave me the right to do whatever I thought was best with what was inside."

Her expression was as cold as granite. "And that makes

you what? My *keeper*? Well, think again. I'm not some naive wallflower that you can manipulate however you see fit. Doug wrote that letter to me, and he obviously wanted me to—"

"Doug left it in that box because he knew I wouldn't give it to you," Tanner argued. "He wrote it for some reason of his own. But he knew me, Cassie. He knew I'd never let you be hurt like that."

"Hurt?" She shook her head. "That doesn't make sense. What's in it that's so terrible?"

"Nothing," Tanner said quietly. "Forget I said—"

"Damn you, Tanner, what did it say?"

The pain and frustration in her voice was unbearable and Tanner fought the urge to take her in his arms. She was breathing hard and her eyes were all fire and rage. But he didn't budge. "I can't tell you."

She stepped closer, toe to toe, her chest heaving. "Oh, yes, you can. And you will. I want to know. *I have a right to know.* I loved him. I had his child. I cried and grieved when he died. So how dare you stand there all arrogant and condescending and with the audacity to tell me that I—"

She loved Doug. That was all he heard.

"Okay," he said, exasperated and frustrated. "Are you sure you want the truth? Because there's no going back once you know. Do you want to know every ugly word?"

"Yes," she said, eyes blazing and defiant.

Tanner drew in a sharp breath. "Okay, Cassie. He wasn't coming back!"

She frowned. "I don't—"

"Even if he'd survived that mission. He had no intention of returning. He didn't want you," Tanner said flatly. "He didn't want the baby. And he wasn't coming back to Crystal Point."

She rocked back on her heels. "I don't believe it," she whispered.

"I'm not lying to you," he said wearily.

Her head shook. "But how could it be true? He never said anything like that to me. He only said we'd talk when he got back." She stopped and looked at him. "He *was* intending to come home. I know it. Perhaps you misunderstood what he—"

"I didn't misunderstand," Tanner said quickly. "When it came to Doug I could guess exactly how he was going to react even before he said or did anything."

Cassie's arms dropped to her sides. "Perhaps he was under pressure and feeling stressed when he wrote it? If he'd talked about it and discussed things…it would have been different. He would have…" She stopped speaking and met his gaze. There was pain and disbelief, and then a sharp realization in her expression. She sighed. "Oh, of course. He did talk, didn't he? He talked to *you*. You've known all along…before you read the letter?"

"I knew," Tanner said softly and nodded. "Doug called me one morning just after you told him you were pregnant."

"But he didn't want to talk to me? He didn't want to discuss it?"

"I don't think so."

She sighed heavily and moved to the sofa. "He didn't want me?" Her words were hollow. "He really didn't want me? He didn't want our baby?"

Tanner knew she was hurting. "I'm sorry…no."

"Who does that?" she asked, looking broken and hopeless. "What kind of man behaves that way…"

"A selfish one," he said and swallowed hard. "But you knew that, Cassie. You dated him for three years. You knew Doug was self-absorbed. You just chose not to see it."

She looked down into her lap for a moment, hands twisted, heart clearly broken. Then she took a deep breath and met his gaze. "You told me the safety deposit box was empty. You lied to me. And you knew this all along and yet you didn't tell me?"

"I couldn't."

She shook her head. "You knew when you arrived here weeks ago and you didn't say anything to me. You let me think he'd had every intention of coming back and that he wanted us. You simply let me believe it and didn't say a word. Not even after we…" Her words trailed and she blinked, batting moisture from her eyes. "We made love and you didn't say a word. Even after that you're still protecting him."

Tanner's chest heaved. She was so wrong. "No, Cassie… I was protecting you."

Cassie was numb all over. She couldn't think or see anything other than Tanner's deliberate intentions to keep the truth from her. Doug wasn't coming back to Crystal Point. He was going to do exactly what he'd done before…bail.

It should have crushed her. But it didn't.

Tanner's lies did.

He might have it all tied up in some neat little package of wanting to spare her feelings, but all he'd done was prove he couldn't be relied upon. He couldn't be trusted.

"I don't need protecting," she said coldly. "All I ever wanted or needed from you was the truth."

"I'm sorry, Cassie. I knew Doug—"

"This isn't about Doug!" she snapped and got to her feet. "Don't you get it? This is about you. Me. *Us.* This is about you making the decision to lie to me, to treat me like I'm some kind of weakling who can't handle real life. Well, I'm not," she said, getting madder with each passing second. "I'm not weak. I'm not emotionally frail. And I'm not a pushover. And right now all I feel like is the world's most gullible fool for believing that you could be trusted. When clearly, you can't."

Every ounce of rage and disappointment in her heart rose to the surface. All her life she'd felt as if she wasn't quite equal to the task of standing on her own two feet. After her parents died her grandfather and her friends had lovingly wrapped her in cotton wool and tried to keep her from enduring more loss and hurt. But in doing that she'd become dependent, avoided making any major decisions and constantly ducked confrontation. Through school. In work. In life. When her grandfather went into the home and the house sold she had stayed on, avoiding change and disruption, accepting the easy road. And she'd become involved with Doug for the same reason. He didn't demand anything. He didn't treat her like a partner. He kept her locked in her gilded cage. Just as her grandfather had. And that's why she'd blindly accepted his continued lack of commitment to their relationship. It was easy. Uncomplicated. *Safe.*

When all she'd really done, over and over, was settle for the easy road.

Even when Oliver came along she hadn't truly grown up to take responsibility for herself and her son. She'd stayed in the house, hoping and avoiding the inevitable. It was a sobering realization and not one she was proud of.

But over the past few weeks things had changed. She'd changed. Because of Tanner.

For the first time in her life someone challenged her. Defied her. Made her feel up to the task and treated her like an equal.

Except it was all a lie.

He'd done the same as everyone else. And worse. Because she'd trusted him.

"I want you to go."

"Cassie, I think we should talk. I know—"

"No," she said angrily. "I don't want to hear it. I don't want to hear about how you didn't tell me for my own good, or how you didn't want me to get hurt, or how you think lying to me is acceptable. It's not. We made love," she said, her voice breaking. "You asked me to marry you. You said you cared about me and Oliver. Those things override anything else. And I don't want to be with someone who thinks it's okay to lie to me about something so important. I'll get over Doug not wanting me or Oliver," she said, her throat so tight it was almost closed. "But I can't get over—"

"So, Doug gets a free pass," he said harshly, interrupting her. "And I don't."

She nodded. "That's right."

He laughed then. Not with humor, but with a kind of weary, resigned acceptance. "Then I guess that tells me everything I need to know."

"I guess it does."

He stared at her, into her, through her. "Goodbye, Cassie."

Then he left. And she dropped onto the sofa and sobbed.

Cassie was thankful she had Oliver and the task of packing up her belongings to keep her mind off her troubles. She hadn't seen or heard from Tanner in six days. She didn't even know if he was still in town. The Realtor had brought a few prospective buyers through the house and each time she'd died a tiny death. Afterward, she'd quickly picked herself up and got back to the job of being strong and resilient and determined to stand on her own.

But she missed him. She missed him so much she ached inside.

And then she remembered that he'd lied to her and betrayed her and the anger returned. Not even Lauren and M.J. could budge her from her feelings. Both women made it clear they thought she was being unforgiving and stubborn. But she would not be swayed. It was over. And it was time she acted like a responsible thirty-one-year-old single mother and stopped whining. It was time to grow up.

But he came by early on Monday morning. She was in the front room and she saw his car pull up outside. She watched as he got out and walked across the lawn. He looked so good. Her heart raced at the sight of him. And then broke just a little bit more. He wore jeans, a dark shirt and leather jacket. He looked handsome and familiar and the memory of every kiss, every touch, came rushing back. He stood at the edge of the garden for a moment and stared out along the street before he pulled the for-sale sign out of the ground. She knew immediately what it meant.

It's done… It's sold…

It's over…

He laid the sign flat in the garden bed and then walked up the path. Cassie pushed some blood into her legs and met him at the front door. She didn't say a word. Neither did he. She headed back into the lounge and waited.

He looked tired. He looked as if he'd been through hell and back. She fought every impulse she possessed to keep herself from rushing into his arms. Too much had been said. There was too much regret and recrimination. He'd go back to South Dakota and forget all about her. And she'd forget him. Someday.

"You sold the house?"

"Not in the way you might think. I have something for you," he said as he pulled an envelope from his jacket pocket and dropped it onto the coffee table. It was a large manila envelope that looked official and had Oliver's name on the front.

"What is it?"

He didn't move. "As it turns out there was some money from Doug's estate. More than we'd first thought. From a new insurance policy Doug had taken out just before he was killed," he said. "Once all the debtors had been paid there was enough left."

Cassie frowned. "Enough for what?"

He waved a hand vaguely. "Enough for this. The deeds for the house are in there, put in trust for Oliver until he's twenty-one. As his mother and legal guardian you now decide what is to be done with the house. So you can stay, or sell…or do whatever you want to."

Cassie's legs were numb. He had to be joking. "I don't understand. How can that be? There was nothing left. Doug hadn't—"

"It was a new policy," he replied flatly. "Like I said. The lawyers missed it at first because it wasn't in the original will. Anyway, it means you can stay here. You can raise Oliver in this house. Which is what you wanted, right?"

The old Cassie had wanted that. But now she couldn't be certain of anything. It was tempting, that's for sure. The house had been her home for such a long time and was filled with memories. It was a safe harbor. Like an old glove that fit her hand perfectly. But she'd also promised herself she'd stand on her own feet.

It was too much to take in and she sat down heavily. "I never thought something like this would happen."

"A lot of things happen we don't expect," he said, still not flinching.

The meaning of his words burned through her entire body. She hadn't expected to fall in love with Tanner McCord. But she had. She hadn't expected to become his lover and long for him in ways she'd never wanted anyone before. But it was for nothing. They were a pipe dream. There were too many obstacles. She knew that Tanner would always feel Doug between them. He'd drawn the line in the sand when he'd decided to deceive her. There was no going back from that.

"I think I'm in shock," she said softly. "Don't get me wrong, I'm happy that my son will be looked after. And I guess this means that if it was a new policy, then maybe Doug did plan to…" She stopped and shrugged. "I don't know what it means or why he did it, but perhaps he wasn't only always thinking of himself. Maybe he did think about us and the baby I was carrying."

"That's probably it," Tanner said and shrugged. "Anyway, I just wanted to let you know."

She tried to smile and failed. Her bottom lip trembled. "So…what now?"

He shrugged again. "I'm flying out on Wednesday."

He was leaving. Going home. Ending things in the most final way possible.

"I see. Well, have a safe trip."

He nodded fractionally. "I'd like to say goodbye to Oliver."

"Sure."

Once he'd left the room Cassie let out a long breath. Her hands shook and she clutched them tightly together. Nothing had ever hurt so much.

Several minutes later he reappeared in the doorway. His back was straight. His face a stony mask. There was such finality in his demeanor. She knew they were over.

"Goodbye, Cassandra."

She didn't move. "Goodbye, Tanner."

And then he was gone. Out of her house. Out of her life. For good.

Chapter Thirteen

Cassie fell back into a post-Tanner rhythm way too easily. But she knew she was behaving like a complete fraud. Of course, she wasn't about to admit it to anyone. Not even her friends. They seemed to believe her happy smiles well enough and no one appeared to guess that she was broken inside.

The house deeds still remained on the coffee table, where Tanner had left them. The soft cotton T-shirt he'd left by the bed was unmoved. Oliver seemed a little quieter than usual and even Mouse acted as though he missed him.

She was, in a word, miserable.

He'd breezed into her life, made her fall in love with him and then breezed out again.

If she wasn't so brokenhearted she'd be madder than hell at him.

Then she got her period and discovering she wasn't

pregnant had her crying for two days. It was silly. She'd never believed she might be. But still…the idea of having Tanner's baby made her remember what she'd had at her fingertips and then lost.

M.J. had unexpectedly gone north to help a friend who needed a hand running her boutique for a few weeks, but Lauren came and went at regular intervals, checking up, making sure she wasn't becoming a boring recluse with only her baby for company. She assured her friend she wasn't, but doubted Lauren believed her. She should have been happy. She had her son and her home. She had what she thought she wanted. But she was unhappier than she'd ever been in her life. The house gave her no comfort. Of course she was happy that Oliver had his legacy and his future was secure. But it was a hollow victory.

Lauren and Gabe helped celebrate her birthday and she put on her bravest face, even though her heart was broken.

And then five weeks after he left Crystal Point she had an unexpected visitor.

Ruthie Nevelson.

"We need to talk" was all she said, and Cassie quickly ushered her inside.

Once they reached the living room Ruthie spoke again.

"This is a nice home," she said and crossed her thin arms. "I can see why it means so much to you."

"It used to belong to my grandfather," she explained, feeling the other woman's scrutiny down to her toes. "When he was ailing we had to sell it so that he could afford full-time care."

"And that's when Doug bought the place, isn't it?"

She nodded. "That's right."

"I'm not sure why he wanted to do that," Ruthie said and shrugged. "It's not like he ever wanted to put down roots.

Maybe it was guilt. Maybe it was a way to stay connected to this town. I guess we'll never know."

Cassie tried to be casual, tried not to let Ruthie see that she was so wound up she could barely string words together. The older woman was Tanner's greatest ally and she had come for a reason. Only, Cassie had no idea what that was. But she got the sense she was about to find out.

"Ruthie, is there something that—"

"I have something for you," she said and pulled a narrow envelope from her small handbag. "Actually, it's for your son. It's a letter from Tanner."

Cassie took the envelope with shaking fingers. "What does it say?"

Ruthie shrugged. "I don't know. But knowing Tanner, I would guess that it's from the heart."

Cassie swallowed hard. "What should I do with it?"

"Read it yourself. Or give it to him when he's old enough to understand," Ruthie said and paced the room. When she reached the mantel she looked at the photographs. Then she turned and made an impatient sound. "I encouraged Tanner to go home, you know. I saw how deeply he was getting involved with you and tried to stay impartial. But I couldn't. And I can't understand why you would want to waste time hanging on to the ghost of a man who wasn't worthy of either of you."

Cassie's shoulders dropped. "It isn't about Doug."

"Of course it is," Ruthie said and tutted. "You and Tanner have been on a collision course since the day his brother bought this house."

"What did Tanner tell you?"

"Enough," she replied. "That he asked you to marry him. That you turned him down."

"I didn't," Cassie said quickly. "I mean, not exactly. We

had an argument and in the heat of everything that was said it was all kind of forgotten."

"Well, I'm pretty sure he didn't do any forgetting," Ruthie said and frowned. "Do you have any idea of what that boy has done for you? What he's sacrificed so that you and your son can have a safe home?"

Cassie stared at Ruthie. "What? I don't understand what you—"

The older woman sighed crossly. "No, I guess you don't. Well, it's high time you learned exactly what kind of man Tanner McCord is."

"I know what he is," she said dully. "But I also know he kept the truth from me. He lied by omission."

"Yes," Ruthie said tersely. "He did. And he shouldn't have. He should have told you what a no-good lout Doug McCord was from the very beginning. But he's too decent, too honorable to *dishonor* his brother that way."

"That's no excuse. He was wrong. And he wouldn't admit it. He wouldn't stop being arrogant and bullheaded and thinking he knew what was best for me. And in the end it didn't matter what was in the letter Doug wrote because there was an insurance policy that—"

"Nonsense," Ruthie said and waved her hands. "There was no insurance. No anything. Doug made sure of that. All he left was a pile of debt and a child he had no intention of claiming." The older woman sat down. "You're not that naive. In your heart you know everything you found out about Doug is true. The lies, the betrayal and the way he stole Tanner's inheritance and frittered it away. And then the terrible way he treated Leah."

Cassie clutched her sides. "I know that. I know Doug wasn't perfect. But what does that have to do with this house. Tanner said there was an insurance policy and I—"

"He took out a second mortgage on his ranch," Ruthie

said, cutting her off. "And that's how you got to keep this house."

Silence consumed the room. Cassie dropped into the chair by the window. It couldn't be true. He wouldn't do that. It was impossible. Tears grew hot behind her eyes and she met the other woman's gaze. "But…I don't understand. Why would he do that?"

Ruthie shook her head with clear exasperation. "Because, you foolish girl, *he loves you.*"

Cassie swallowed the lump in her throat. It was too much. Too hard to grasp.

He loves you…

"I don't think—"

"And he loves your baby," Ruthie added. "Frankly, I don't think I've ever seen a man as much in love as Tanner is with both of you."

Cassie was too stunned to move as she tried to absorb what she'd just learned. "But…he never said… He never said he felt that way. When he proposed he talked about Oliver and how we were good together, how we made sense. But there was no mention of him being…of feeling…of loving me. Why wouldn't he—"

"Lay his heart on the line?" Ruthie inquired, eyes wide. "Oh, I don't know. Perhaps it had something to do with you being in love with his brother?"

"But I'm not," she insisted hotly and got to her feet. "I don't feel that way about Doug…not anymore. And I don't think I ever really did. I cared about him and loved him in a way. But not like I love…"

She stopped, feeling Ruthie's questioning glance down to the soles of her feet.

"Go on," Ruthie prompted. "Say it."

Cassie took a deep breath and sighed. "Not like I love Tanner."

Ruthie smiled. "Well, good for you. And now that's out in the open, what are you going to do about it?"

Cassie was still thinking about the other woman's words long after she'd left.

He loves you...

Did he? Had she been so foolish? So blind? He'd never mentioned love. He cared, that's what he said. They were good together, in bed and out of it. They could give Oliver a home...a family.

Love hadn't rated a mention.

If it had...

Would she have responded differently? Would she have found it in her heart to forgive him?

So, Doug gets a free pass and I don't...

There was anger in his voice when he'd said the words. And regret. And pain.

And still she hadn't budged. She'd remained stubborn and resolute. Determined to think the worst. To blame him. To make him suffer. For what? Doug's sins? If so, what did that make her? A scared, confused little girl who'd been duped and wanted to lash out at the one person she'd subconsciously believed would take it and not bail on her? Would not leave her? Would not abandon her?

The realization hit home with the force of a sledge-hammer.

Doug's letter was exactly the excuse she'd needed to push Tanner away.

The intensity of her feelings for him had terrified her and once she'd been dealt an out clause she'd grabbed it with both hands. Like a coward. Like the girl who'd never had to stand on her own two feet.

But she wasn't that girl anymore. She was a woman. And it was about time she started acting like one. She took a breath, grabbed the letter Ruthie had given her and opened it. Tanner's neat handwriting jumped out and she shuddered with emotion as she started reading.

Dear Oliver,

I'm not sure how old you'll be when you read this. Hopefully old enough to understand what I'm saying. I just wanted you to know about your dad. He was a lot older than me so we didn't spend much time together when I was young. But he was always there, always happy to play games and be a great big brother. He had his faults but he was a brave soldier and gave his life for his country. I want you to know that if he were here he'd teach you all the things our father taught us...like how to ride a horse and fix a fence. And how to be honest and honorable and try to always do what's right, even if you know someone might get hurt.

It's not easy growing up without your dad around. I know because I lost my dad, too, when I was young. But just know that if your dad had been here he would be very proud that you're his son. I can't promise I'll always be around for you, but if you ever need me you can trust that I will be there. I'll be here for you to talk to, to ask questions or simply to listen.

Being around you and your mom reminded me what it was like to be part of a family and I love you both more than I can say.

Tanner

Cassie clutched the letter, tears streaming down her face. And she knew, for the first time in her life, what she wanted. And who. She grabbed the telephone and called Ruthie. A few minutes later she had the details she needed.

She checked the clock. It was late in South Dakota. But not too late. Once she dialed it took several seconds and then a deep, unfamiliar voice answered.

"Hi," she said and drew in a breath, feeling stronger than she had in a long time. In forever. "My name is Cassie Duncan. And I need your help."

Tanner stretched out his shoulders and gripped the saddle in his hands. He was tired. He couldn't remember the last time he'd slept through the night.

Liar...

The last time he'd slept more than four hours had been when he'd had Cassie's arms wrapped around him. They'd made love and afterward he'd fallen asleep with her curled up against his chest. He missed making love with her. He missed her so much he ached all over. And he missed Oliver.

But he was right to leave.

He wasn't going to beg for her and act like a fool any more than he already had. He had his fair share of pride and she'd battered his ego with a shovel. She couldn't forgive him. And she didn't care enough to try. Besides, she'd made it abundantly clear that her feelings were still with his brother.

I loved him. I had his child. I cried and grieved when he died.

"Everything all right?"

Grady Parker's voice thrust him back into the present. His best friend was looking at him, one brow up. "Sure," he said and rested the saddle. "Fine."

He'd been at his friend's ranch most of the morning, cutting out the older calves from a large herd of Charolais cattle while Grady and his foreman took some of the steers to market.

"Any chance you can ride down to the pasture behind Flat Rock and check out the mustangs? They've been down by the watering hole most of the week, but I'm pretty sure there's a roan filly that's lame. Might be worth you looking at her before I call the vet out."

Flat Rock was a thirty-minute ride, but still part of Grady's land. The Parker ranch was one of the biggest and oldest in the county and butted his place along the edge of the creek. Tanner didn't really feel like a one-hour round-trip but knew his friend was right. And the filly needed to be looked at.

"Yeah, no problem."

Grady nodded. "Great. I gotta head into town for an errand so if I'm not back just leave Solo in the corral."

Solo was Grady's mild-tempered paint gelding. A horse that Tanner had broken in a few years earlier and had been riding that morning. "Okay."

His friend moved to leave, then hesitated for a moment. "You sure you're okay? You've only been riding again for a couple of weeks. If it's too much I can—"

"Stop worrying like an old woman, will you?" he said and tucked the saddle on his hip. "I'm fine. The leg's not giving me much trouble and I'm good to ride."

Grady lingered for a second and then shrugged. "Okay. I'm taking the girls with me," he said about his three young daughters. "And thanks for your help today."

Tanner waved the other man off and grabbed Solo's gear. Once he was tacked up he swung into the saddle and headed off. The trail to Flat Rock was well-worn and he eased the gelding into a steady trot for most of the way. Ten minutes in and he knew a solitary ride was exactly what he needed to clear his mind.

If that were possible. He spent most of his days and nights thinking about Cassie. Wondering how he'd made such a mess of it all. He loved her…but he hadn't the courage to say the words. He wanted her, but he'd been unwilling to stay around and play second fiddle to his brother.

He had to get her out of his head. And his heart.

Once he reached Flat Rock and the mustangs, he singled out the filly and took a short video on his cell. She did appear to be slightly lame and he texted Grady to get the vet out when he had the chance.

By the time he got back to the ranch it was past two o'clock. Grady hadn't returned from his trip to town, so Tanner unsaddled Solo and left him in the corral and headed for his truck. It was a short trip back to his ranch and he slowed as he drove beneath the wide white gates. Two *M*'s entwined on the logo and he let out a long breath. He'd called the ranch The Double M, hoping that one day he'd have someone to share it with. For the briefest moment he'd thought that someone was Cassie.

But he was wrong.

The gravel driveway was long and straight and he spotted a vehicle parked out front of the house. As he got closer he realized it was Grady's dual-cab truck. And his friend was resting against the back, arms crossed, hat slung low over his forehead.

Tanner pulled the truck to a halt and got out.

"What are you doing here?" he asked and noticed that his friend's daughters were in the backseat.

Grady jerked his head to one side in the direction of the house. "See for yourself."

Tanner turned his gaze to the farmhouse and stood motionless. A dog sat on the porch. A huge black-and-white dog he'd recognize anywhere. Mouse.

It's not possible…

The door opened and a figure emerged.

Cassie.

His heart thundered in his chest. His legs wouldn't move. His skin felt as if it was on fire. He saw her walk onto the porch and still he didn't want to allow himself to believe it.

He glanced toward Grady, who had now pushed himself off the rear of the truck and was grinning.

Grady tapped him on the shoulder. "Go get your family."

Tanner stood motionless, unable to move his legs. She was near the porch step, her beautiful hair flowing around her shoulders. He tried to move and failed. It was only when he heard Grady's truck pulling away that he gathered the strength to shift his limbs. He walked across the yard, his chest so tight he felt as though his heart might burst through his rib cage.

When he reached the bottom step he stopped. Mouse, who was tethered to a railing, whined and wagged his long tail. Tanner heard a baby laugh from inside the front door. Oliver. His heart rolled over.

"Hi," she said softly.

Tanner met her gaze. "Hello."

She took a deep breath. "You left something behind."

Tanner's insides jumped. "I did? What?"

She exhaled heavily. "Me. Us."

"Cassie, I…" His words trailed. He wanted to take her in his arms. He wanted to feel her kiss and her sweet touch. But first, he had to be sure. "Why are you here?"

She stared at him, her eyes glistening. "Your friend Grady is a nice man. He picked us up from the airport yesterday and we stayed at a motel in town."

His brows came up. Grady had some explaining to do. "You got on an airplane?"

She nodded. "My first. I've been doing a lot of things

for the first time lately. I started taking real responsibility for myself and my son. And I got a backbone, too."

He smiled a little. "And what do you intend to do with it?"

Her shoulders pushed back. "Fight for what I want."

"And what's that?"

Her mouth curved and she moved closer to the edge of the step. "You."

Tanner sucked in a breath. He wanted to believe her. He wanted it more than he'd wanted anything in his life. But resistance lingered. He didn't want to get his hopes up. Didn't want to have her for a moment only to lose her again.

"That's not how you felt a month ago."

"I'm not the same woman I was a month ago," she said quietly, moving onto the lower step. "I've changed. Knowing you has changed me." She paused and took a steadying breath. "I know about the house. I know what you did." She dropped onto the next step down. "But I would never have stood for it."

She was closer. Almost touching distance. "It's what you wanted. What you'd hoped for. You love that house. You grew up there. Why does it matter how it came about?"

"Because it does matter." She swept her gaze around the yard. "What if something happened and you lost all of this, because of me? I couldn't bear it."

"Money and possessions have never been important to me, Cassie. You should know that by now."

"I do know," she said and took another step closer. "It's one of the reasons why I…why I feel the way I do about you."

His heart stopped beating. Was that her roundabout way of saying she loved him? "You love Doug."

She shook her head. "I *loved* Doug. Once…a lifetime

ago. Before I knew you. Before I realized what it was to be with someone who is my friend...and my lover...and my truest soul mate."

"Cassie, I can't—"

"Don't say no to me," she implored, her face all emotion, her blue eyes glittering brightly. "Not when I came all this way to tell you how I feel about you."

Tanner's throat closed over. "Then tell me."

Her breath caught. "I'm in love with you."

And there it was. All he needed to hear. All he wanted. Her heart. Her love. "You're sure?"

She nodded. "Never surer. I love that you make me smile in one moment and make me mad the next. I love that you make love to me so passionately that I feel like the most desirable woman in the world. And I love how you love Oliver, and I want to make him all over again with you."

Tanner quickly took the two last steps and met her halfway. "I love you, too," he whispered against her mouth before he kissed her. "So very much."

She kissed him back and Tanner wrapped his arms around her. Feeling her close as if she was the air in his lungs.

Finally she pulled back a little and placed her hands on his shoulders. "I read the letter you wrote to Oliver. I knew as I read the words that you would always be there for him. That you would always love him and protect him. And I couldn't ask for a better father for my son. And the children I'm going to have with you in the future."

"And Doug?" he asked quietly.

"A memory," she replied. "And the person who brought us together, even if that was never his intention."

Tanner touched her face. "I will love you all the days of

my life, Cassie. You were the first girl I kissed." He smiled, cradling her cheek. "And you'll be the last."

She smiled. "You can bet your boots on that score, cowboy."

Oliver made a sound and Tanner tensed. "Where is he?"

"In the hall, in his stroller. He's missed you so much."

"I've missed him, too. And you." He linked an arm around her waist and they walked up the steps. "I've even missed this goofy dog of yours."

"Our dog now," she said and smiled.

"And our son," he said as they moved into the hall and noticed Oliver waving his hands excitedly from his stroller. A minute later they were in the living room, side by side on the dark leather sofa, and Tanner had Oliver in his arms. "He's grown so much," he said, bouncing him gently.

Cassie curled against him. "You really are remarkable with him. He sleeps and eats much better for you than me." She smiled and her eyes lit up. "I can't wait to have more children. The ranch and this house are so big and roomy, it should be filled with half a dozen kids."

Tanner laughed. "Six kids? I better get a second job."

She stroked his arm and smiled. "No need. The house in Crystal Point has just gone under contract. It's sold and the money will pay off the second mortgage you foolishly but adorably took out on the ranch." He went to protest but she placed her fingertips against his mouth. "I won't negotiate on this, Tanner. It's done."

"You took something of a risk, selling the house and coming here."

She shrugged. "I've turned over a new leaf. I needed to go after what I wanted. I've never done that before." She squeezed his thigh. "But it feels good. And I think I'm going to want to get my own way a whole lot more in the future."

He laughed. It was the first time he'd done that in weeks. "I think I like this new leaf of yours. It's very...sexy."

"Good, get used to it. I'm not a pushover anymore."

Tanner raised a skeptical brow. "Since when were you ever a pushover?"

"Well, not with you," she said. "But with other people. With Doug...I'm ashamed to say I put up with things. It was easy. No pressure. No risk. When we first met I was at a genuinely low ebb. My grandfather had gone into full-time care and I'd recently been overlooked for a promotion in my job. And then he showed up, all smiles and charm. And we sort of fell into it. He only came around to check out the house he'd bought and to meet the tenant. He certainly didn't intend on staying. I don't think he intended having a girlfriend, either."

Tanner nodded. "He was always more at home with his military colleagues than he was with his civilian life."

She smiled agreeably and without any lingering look of heartache. "I know. And when we were together there weren't any fireworks or bells and banjos or that kind of thing. It wasn't particularly passionate, either, if you get my meaning. It was simply...easy. And when he came home every now and then, I had a boyfriend and he had someone to look after his needs."

Tanner swallowed hard. "You don't have to justify your relationship with him to me."

"I know. But I think that's why I found it so confusing to be around you," she admitted. "When you came to visit that first time I was surprised by how aware of you I was. Doug had told me you were this moody and disinterested loner who liked horses better than people, and when I met you all I felt was this intense attraction. I couldn't get a handle on it. And I felt guilty. I knew I shouldn't have been secretly lusting after you when I considered myself to be in a relationship with your brother."

He chuckled. "Ah—that's why you ignored me?"

She nodded. "You did a fair amount of ignoring yourself."

"I know. I remembered who you were straightaway and I was knocked for a loop. And then I got to know you a little and all I could think was that my brother had somehow got the woman *I* was meant to be with to love him."

"So you stayed away?"

"Yes," he said.

"Until Doug was killed?"

Tanner sighed heavily. "I knew what he'd planned. I knew he hadn't the intention or foresight to make things right. And I was tired of being angry at him. I wanted it over. I wanted to make sure Oliver had what was rightfully his so I could move on." He met her gaze. "Except after two days with you I realized I was kidding myself."

"Two days?" Her eyes glittered. "You knew you loved me after two days?"

"Absolutely."

"I had no idea," she said.

"I did ask you to marry me, remember?"

She grimaced. "I know. But I thought you asked me because of Oliver and because we're...you know...good in bed together."

He grinned. "Well, that was certainly part of it. But I asked you to marry me because I love you. I was just too afraid to say it."

She pressed against him. "I wasn't much better. I'm so happy it's all out in the open now. There's nothing between us now."

"Cassie, about Doug's letter," he said, a little more soberly. "Have you forgiven me for keeping it from you?"

She nodded. "There was nothing to forgive. I know you only wanted to protect me and in some way protect Doug, too. Once I got over my stubborn childishness I understood."

Tanner sighed and grasped her hand, linking their fingers. "He wasn't all bad, you know. While he did some questionable things, like all of us he had his own demons to deal with. He was never the same after our parents died."

"He gave me Oliver," she said and sighed.

"He gave me my family," Tanner said and marveled at the woman and child he was holding in his arms. "And I'll always be grateful for that."

She pressed even closer and kissed him. "Does that mean you're going to ask me to marry you again?"

Tanner smiled. "Pushy, eh?"

"Just curious," she replied and grinned. "And I am up for trying new things these days."

Tanner moved, placed Oliver in his stroller, and then he dropped to his knees in front of her.

"Marry me, Cassandra?" he asked quietly. "Marry me and let me love you for the rest of our days," he said, proposing for a second time to the woman he loved.

And this time she said yes.

Epilogue

Cassie was sure she'd forgotten something. She had her something old—a pendant that had been her mother's—and her something blue was an exquisite lace handkerchief that Ruthie had gifted her.

I'm getting married today...

Their wedding was to be a simple ceremony at the courthouse with a justice of the peace and then dinner at the O'Sullivan pub down on Dryer Street. She was getting married, four weeks and one day after she'd arrived in Cedar Creek. She'd fallen in love with the small town, with its wide streets and unique mix of old and new storefronts. And she'd fallen in love with Tanner a little bit more every day.

And although they were doing everything fast, Lauren, Gabe and M.J. had flown in for the wedding. As had Ruthie.

"You look so beautiful."

Cassie turned from her spot near the bedroom window and saw Tanner in the doorway. "And you're not supposed to see the bride before the wedding."

He put a hand to his heart. "I promise it'll be our little secret."

Cassie smiled lovingly. He looked so handsome in his dark suit. She never tired of admiring him. And she knew it was mutual. "If M.J. catches you in here you'll be in big trouble."

"She's on the phone in the kitchen yelling at her boyfriend, so I'm off the hook."

Cassie laughed. "She doesn't have a boyfriend."

"So you say," he said and stepped into the room. "She's down there calling some poor guy an arrogant jerk and telling him she never wants to see him again." His eyes darkened with delight. "Sounds like love to me."

"Poor M.J.," Cassie said and grabbed her small rose bouquet. "Well, since you've seen me there's no backing out now."

"No chance," he said and looked her over. "You look amazing."

Cassie had chosen a knee-length ivory chiffon dress with a beautiful beaded bodice and pearl-colored heels. Her hair was down, her makeup minimal and the ring on her finger felt as though it had been there forever. They'd chosen it together from a small jewelry store in town. It was an antique setting with perfect white stones set in platinum. It wasn't huge or ostentatious. It was elegant and understated and exactly what she'd dreamed of.

"You know, you could have had a big fancy wedding with all the trappings," he said, and not for the first time since he'd proposed.

"I know," she replied. "But this is what I wanted. Just you and me and Oliver surrounded by the people we really care about. And you know how I love the steaks at the O'Sullivan pub," she said and laughed.

"Even without the finest Parker Charolais beef on the table," he said, grinning. "Who doesn't?"

Grady's brother-in-law owned the pub and it was no secret the two men barely tolerated one another. "So, how about you go and grab our little angel and we'll get going."

"He's with Ruthie. So, for the next—" he checked his watch "—ten minutes, you're all mine, Miss Duncan."

She smiled lovingly. "Soon-to-be Mrs. McCord."

He moved closer and reached for her hand, and then kissed her knuckles softly. "I can't wait."

"Me, either," she said with complete love in her heart. "I love you."

He grinned, but Cassie wasn't fooled. He was as moved by emotion as she was.

"I love you, too."

And an hour later they were in front of the justice of the peace, declaring their love and devotion to one another. Cassie cried a little during the ceremony as Tanner spoke of loving and honoring her for all his life. Once their vows were made and their marriage officiated, Tanner gripped her hand, took Oliver in the crook of one arm and led them out of the courthouse and onto the front steps.

And into the rest of their lives.

* * * * *

0115_INSHIP